The Gangster underworld
Undercover Gangster
Part one

Blood Ties in the Shadows

Joseph Jethro

First published in Great Britain in 2024
ISBN: 978-1-917452-11-3

josephjethro45@outlook.com

Chapter 1
The Unseen Path

Ramello sat on his bed; his curtains closed, and the only light was the plasma's soft blue hue. He watched a video of himself when he was speeding on Channelside Drive last week. The wind had whipped through his hair, the thrill of speeding making him go even faster, but fate had a way of catching up, and it did in the form of flashing lights and a stern-faced officer. He got a hefty fine of five hundred dollars. He winced at the memory, but there was a satisfaction in watching it unfold on screen. He enjoyed watching about himself; it was better than a movie. As the video played on, he couldn't move his eyes away. The reckless joy of speeding and the fear of getting caught was such a lovely thrill for him. Ramello leaned back, lost in the drama of his own making, 'Better than any movie,' he whispered to the empty room.

'Ramello!' one of his adoptive parent's sons shouted from downstairs, 'Get down here right away.'

Ramello sighed, switched his plasma off and headed down the stairs, his footsteps echoing with every step. He found his brothers in the living room. He didn't have an actual brother and was known for being abandoned as a baby. Then, someone did adopt him, but unfortunately, he died a few years ago, leaving behind his three sons and his adopted son, Ramello. Ramello's brothers were older than him and were always horrible to him.

'What is it, Frederik?' Ramello asked his brother, who had called him downstairs.

'I just wanted to ask how far you got in paying your fine off?' Frederik asked in frustration.

'I paid it off last night,' Ramello replied swiftly, 'Why are you so interested in my business anyway?'

'Cause I don't want any more of your rubbish letters cluttering the doorstep,' Frederik responded with a smirk, leaning against the door frame, 'And make sure you don't get any more fines. We don't want any more rubbish.'

Ramello sighed and walked over to the drawer where he had placed his car key. He picked it up and was about to walk out when Phillip, sitting across the room, asked, 'Are you planning to go car racing again and get more fines coming through the door?'

'Yeah, I am,' Ramello replied, rolling his hazel eyes as he left the room.

He stormed out of the front door towards his black sports car, a slick ride, and jumped in. He started the engine and sped out of the driveway. The vehicle accelerated, and the world blurred around him. The fines and the letters all faded into oblivion.

He sped along the road; the mild breeze tousled his brown hair as he rolled the window down.

He parked his car on a narrow, desolate street. The cracked asphalt crunched under his trainers as he stepped out, the weight of his stressful and miserable life pressing down on his shoulders. He longed for a way to improve his circumstances, and he definitely wanted to find a way of getting along with his brothers. The warm wind, tinged with dust, tousled his hair, and the bright sun forced him to squint.

As he walked past a sleek silver sedan, its door abruptly swung open, striking his leg and sending him stumbling to the ground. His eyes narrowed in anger and pain as he looked up. To his alarm, five black-clad men emerged from the vehicle. Ramello's pulse quickened, instincts warning him of imminent danger.

'You get here, boy,' one of the men growled, his fingers digging into Ramello's shoulders as he pulled him to his feet and slammed him against a brick wall, 'Where's your dad?'

Ramello looked at the man blankly, trying to get out of his grasp and shouted, 'I don't have a dad. Get off me!'

The other men started to laugh mockingly; the man who had Ramello gripped gave him dirty, terrifying looks and then continued, 'Listen, young man, it's obvious that you have a dad. Tell me right now, where is he?' he yelled impatiently.

'I'm not lying. I was abandoned when I was a baby, and my adoptive father died a few years back,' Ramello replied, his voice firm. He didn't understand what the man was talking about, 'I think you've got the wrong person,' he yelled.

The man's hand slipped under his bomber jacket, pulling out a gleaming black, polished handgun. He pointed the weapon at Ramello's head, 'Listen boy, tell me right now before I shoot you.'

Ramello shivered, 'Look, man, I don't know what you're banging on about, serious man, I don't know!'

The man clenched his teeth, his eyes narrowing into slits, 'I don't want any nonsense to slip out of your mouth; I'm only interested in your dad, and let me make it clear, your actual dad,' he hissed, his voice filled with impatience and frustration.

Ramello shook his head, raising his voice, 'Look man, I don't know if my dad is dead or alive; I only know his name, nothing else; it's the only information I've got.'

The man's finger itched to press the trigger of the gun. 'I only wanna know where he is,' he snapped, yanking his phone from his pocket. He hesitated for a moment and then dialled a number. Someone instantly answered.

'What is it, Richmond?' echoed a voice from the other side of the line, 'I told ya not to call me until the bloody job is done, so have ya cracked it?'

Richmond's grip tightened on the phone, the weight of the gun pressing against Ramello's temple, 'I've got the lad with me. The idiot is not telling me the whereabouts of his dad. He's saying that he doesn't know, he's gotta be lying, maybe I should put a bullet in his head?'

There was a moment of silence. Suddenly, the man on the other line spoke. 'Bring the boy over to ma place,' he lazily instructed, a sense of hatred in his tone. 'I'll talk to him myself.'

Richmond ended the call, his eyes locked onto Ramello who stood angrily confused. Suddenly, he clutched Ramello's arm with a firm, tight grip. He dragged Ramello towards a waiting silver Mercedes-Benz, the car's sleek lines glinting in the sun's light, a stark contrast to the desolate surroundings. Richmond flung open the back door and forcefully shoved Ramello into the vehicle.

Ramello looked around, his thoughts going insane. *What in the world was going on, and who were these weird men?*

Richmond jumped into the driver's seat, glancing at the man who was quietly sitting in the passenger seat. He stared at the road ahead with an unwavering gaze and cracked his knuckles.

Richmond looked back at Ramello with a smirk. 'Be prepared for a long journey, boy,' he declared, and in his voice was a stern warning.

Chapter 2
The Evil Mobster

Ramello slumped back, his back leaning against the leather interior. They had been travelling for ages, and the journey didn't seem to be coming to an end. Everyone in the car was silent.

Suddenly, the man in the front passenger seat broke the silence, 'Did you ask the boy's name, Richie?' he inquired, 'What if you've got the wrong kid?'

'I'm not bloody stupid, Jaylon,' Richmond snapped, his hands tightening on the steering wheel, 'I know the boy's face inside out.'

Jaylon leaned back, his eyes glinting with mischief, 'Have you ever tried to turn the boy's face inside out?' he quipped, sarcasm dripping off every syllable.

Richmond ignored him and sped around a roundabout, earning angry horns from other drivers. Ramello clung to the seat, his knuckles turning white with tension. Richmond then sped through a narrow street and suddenly applied the brake as they entered a grand street with huge mansions.

'We're finally here,' Richmond grumbled under his breath.

He parked in front of the biggest mansion and jumped out, followed by Jaylon. He opened the back door and glared at Ramello, 'Get out of the car!' he ordered, his voice sharp like a blade.

Ramello silently followed the two men into the mansion's garden, a vast expanse of greenery. The driveway was wide, and a metallic black Audi was parked near a garage with clear glass doors. The car's glossy surface reflected the sunlight, hinting at the power concealed within. Inside the garage, a glimmering Lamborghini Aventador could be seen, its body a blend of power and grace. The sleek car seemed to pulse with restrained energy, waiting for the open road. Parked near it was a red SUV, a colossal beast. Its crimson paint seemed defiant, daring anyone to challenge its authority. They walked along a cobblestone pathway, the beds of vibrant blooms stretching in every direction, filling the air with the sweet perfume of jasmine, lavender, and honeysuckle. There was an outdoor dining area, complete with a marble table, a perfect spot for a leisurely meal.

Finally, they arrived at the front door and knocked. The grand door opened swiftly, and there stood a tall man. His jet-black hair cascaded in silky waves, meticulously styled with a daring side fringe that framed his chiselled features. Each strand seemed to hold secrets—dark and mysterious, just like the man himself. His slim-fit black jeans hugged his legs, emphasising his athletic physique, and his jumper clung to his torso. His eyes, oh those eyes, were a mesmerising shade of crimson. Not the ordinary hue of blood but a deeper, more intense red. They held a magnetic allure, drawing people in like moths to a flame. His lips, full and inviting, curved into a half-smile that left hearts fluttering in his wake. And when he spoke, his voice carried a velvety timbre, a blend of danger and seduction that sent shivers down spines. 'Aah! Ya brought ma present. About time!' he said, his voice a velvet whisper.

'Yeah, Red Devil,' Richmond said.

Ramello considered the word 'Devil' as something terrible, yet the figure standing by the grand door remained unperturbed.

'Come in, my guests,' RD beckoned, with an evil grin.

Jaylon pushed Ramello into the mansion, making him stumble. They entered the living room, RD following behind, his footsteps silent.

'Sit on this chair, Ramello,' RD instructed, his smile a blend of charm and menace.

Ramello's mind raced; how did RD know his name? He had arrived at the mansion with nothing but curiosity. Yet, RD had greeted him as if he knew him.

As he lowered himself onto the chair, Ramello's eyes flickered to RD's wrist. There, snug against tanned skin, rested a silver bracelet, a single braided strand that seemed to hold memories of distant lands and whispered promises. Its clasp bore an intricate design, a labyrinth of twists and turns that mirrored the complexities of their situation. But it was the signet ring that captured Ramello's attention most. RD's fingers toyed with it absentmindedly—a polished silver band.

The silver chain around RD's neck was unassuming yet elegant. Its links were delicate, catching the light in a subtle dance. It whispered of memories, whispered promises, and the quiet strength of a man who navigated shadows with grace.

RD circled him, his footsteps tapping silently, 'I seek answers,' he murmured, leaning over Ramello's shoulder, so close he could feel the heat of his breath on his neck, 'I am willing to sacrifice anything and everything to get answers,' he continued.

Ramello, sweating profusely, became extremely worried as he listened to the words coming from RD's mouth. What was the meaning behind these unusual remarks? He wondered stressfully.

Suddenly, Ramello's phone started to ring. RD looked at him, his crimson eyes narrowing with suspicion, 'Who's calling you?' he demanded in a low growl.

Ramello hesitantly took his phone out of his pocket, his hand shaking with fear, 'It's my brother, Edmond,' he stammered.

RD moved closer, his deep breathing sending cold shivers down Ramello's spine. 'Edmond,' he mused, 'Family ties can be both a blessing and a curse.' He swiftly snatched the phone from Ramello's sweaty hands and walked over to a crystalline window, staring at the beautiful horizon; he then answered the call, tilting his head to one side. 'Hello.'

For a moment, there was silence on the other side of the phone, but RD was not a person who tolerated silence, 'Have you got a voice or not? You stupid boy!' he thundered, his voice echoing off the walls.

'Is...is it you, Ramello?' Edmond stammered from the other end of the phone in a worried tone.

'Do I sound like Ramello, boy?' RD asked.

Edmond didn't answer; there was only silence.

'You wanna know who's behind the curtain?' said RD, his voice hissing like a snake, 'Red Devil.'

'Ramello! Can you stop playing games?' shouted Edmond.

RD gave an eerie laugh, 'Ain't nobody messing around with you, and yeah, for your knowledge, I've got your brother trapped in my house, and he ain't coming back alive,' he declared.

'Where's Ramello?' Edmond shouted, 'Whoever you are, you better let him go before I come and gun you down.'

RD laughed hysterically, 'Yo, you're gonna gun me down when ya ain't even got ma coordinates. Meanwhile, I've got your whole crew of brothers scooped out. If you step out of line, I'll slide through and light up you and your two brothers,' he declared in his slangy tone.

Edmond slammed the phone down, leaving RD laughing with satisfaction.

RD turned back to Ramello and threw the phone at him, 'Take that,' he said with a thoughtful face.

Ramello slid it back into his pocket, 'What do you even want from me?' he shouted, the words echoing through the room.

RD brushed his slick, jet-black locks away from his face and smirked, 'And of course, ya don't have an idea why I brought ya here,' he drawled, his voice sharpening quickly, 'Well, let's get to the point then, I want ya to give the game away on where your old man's at.'

'Old man?' Ramello shouted, clenching his teeth, 'What does that mean?'

'It's slang for 'dad', fam,' Jaylon laughed, 'I think you've never been to school before. I guess you've been hiding under a rock all your life.'

'Tell me, where is he?' RD questioned, staring at Ramello and tapping his foot impatiently on the waxed marble.

Ramello's irritation flared, 'What do you want me to say to you? I DON'T KNOW!' he shouted.

RD did not like to be messed around with; he pulled his pistol from his belt holster, the metal cool against his palm. With precision, he cocked it and pointed it at Ramello, 'Step up, young blood,' he taunted, his crimson eyes locking into Ramello's, 'You best tell me if ya wanna vibe with a tranquil, zen life.'

'I told your joey as well,' Ramello's voice wavered, 'I don't have any answers for you.'

RD sighed and put his gun on the desk, 'I guess you really don't know much about your miserable dad then,' he said, his eyes assessing Ramello, 'But that ain't gonna stop me from hunting him down,' he added, a smirk playing on his lips, 'I'm going to get that lowlife, he's a bloody dog, man!'

RD clicked his fingers, and his men seized Ramello's arms and dragged him through the hallway; they opened the front door and, with a forceful motion, flung Ramello out, causing him to fall to his knees.

RD stood sternly overlooking Ramello, who was on the ground, 'You can stroll back to your crib. Ain't no shame in that game,' he laughed mockingly, slamming the door in his face.

Ramello stood up and brushed the dust off his clothes; he didn't understand how he was going to get back home; he was so far away.

He stepped out of the garden and walked down the road, the gravel crunching beneath his shoes.

Fifteen minutes had passed since he had been kicked out of RD's house. He was on the main road when a SUV parked near him. He started scrutinising the car and saw a man sitting in it with another man sitting in the passenger's seat.

The driver rolled down his tinted window, 'Do you need help, lad, you look lost?' he asked with a genuine smile.

Ramello didn't know what to say, 'Yeah, I'm kinda lost,' he finally admitted. 'Don't actually know where I am.'

'Jump in, and I'll take you wherever you want,' said the man, smiling.

Ramello weighed his options. The road ahead was uncertain, but this man didn't look evil like RD. So, he got into the car, RD seemed like a distant nightmare now, and the man's smile held a promise of escape. 'So, where do you want to go?' the man asked.

'I need to get to Tampa Bay,' Ramello replied, his voice urgent.

'Tampa Bay!' the man exclaimed, 'We are so far from there.'

'I know, but I just need to get out of this place as fast as I can,' Ramello said, urgently.

As the countryside blurred past, Ramello's gaze shifted from the winding road to the man behind the wheel. His unease grew when he noticed the man's bulletproof jacket. Scrutinising him, Ramello's eyes fell on a badge tucked into the man's cargo trouser pocket, slightly poking out. The badge bore the words 'Secret Agent,' along with a identification number, and other symbols signifying the officer's authority and responsibilities.

Ramello felt his heart racing; he wondered what he had just gotten into. The officer's frequent glances at the rearview mirror only added to his apprehension, as if he were checking for pursuers.

They drove in silence, when, like a sudden storm, the driver's phone rang. The cop answered, 'What is it, Officer Benjamin?' he asked, his voice steady.

'We need backup immediately, Salvatore,' Officer Benjamin answered in an urgent voice.

Salvatore sighed, his grip on the steering wheel tightening, 'Why does it always have to be me?' he muttered, frustration lacing his words, 'I'm trying to take...' his voice trailed off, then he corrected himself, 'I'm trying to take this lad home, he was lost.'

'Well, there is no time for escorting lost children home; we need to take immediate action,' Officer Benjamin snapped.

Salvatore clenched his jaws and glanced back at Ramello, who was caught between curiosity and fear, 'I'll be at the office in ten minutes,' Salvatore declared, abruptly ending the call. 'Hold on, boy,' he said, the weight of responsibility resting on his shoulders, 'We're in for a big mission.'

Ramello nodded uncomfortably.

Salvatore floored the gas pedal. The car shot forward, tyres screeching along the road. The world outside blurred into streaks of colour as he hurtled down the road, the wind howling through the open windows.

Salvatore suddenly yanked the steering wheel aggressively towards the right side, causing the car to veer sharply. The tyres gripped the pavement as it came to a sudden halt in an alley close to a large police station. 'You stay here, lad,' he said, his accent thick with years of rough living. 'I'll be back in a few minutes.' He slammed the car door shut, the metallic clang echoing off the graffiti-covered walls. But then, doubt flickered in his eyes. He hesitated, fingers gripping the door handle. He opened the door again, meeting Ramello's gaze one last time. 'One piece of advice for you, kid,' he said, 'Don't trust anybody.' He shut the door, leaving Ramello in a whirlwind of thoughts, staring at Salvatore, who rushed with his co-worker towards the looming police station.

Chapter 3
Shadows Of The Dark Alley

Ramello's gaze wandered out of the car window; the passing minutes seemed to stretch into eternity, and Salvatore hadn't yet returned. The sun dipped lower, casting long shadows across the pavement.

Then, like a bolt from the blue, Salvatore hurtled towards the car, panting heavily. His co-worker followed close behind, scrambling into the passenger seat. Salvatore jumped into the driver's seat, slamming the door shut.

'It would be good if we could get the lad home before we go on our mission,' his co-worker suggested, his tone practical.

Salvatore's eyes narrowed, 'Yeah, that's okay with me, Officer Jacob?' he said. 'Our mission is towards Tampa Bay, where the lad lives; we'll drop him off on the way.'

'Oh, yeah!' Officer Jacob mumbled, scratching his head sheepishly, 'Does the kid really live there?'

With a determined twist of the ignition key, Salvatore started the car. The engine roared to life, propelling them forward. The road blurred, and the world outside became a streak of lights and shadows. Ten minutes later, they merged onto a bustling motorway.

Ramello's eyelids drooped. It felt like mere moments of rest, but they were already in Tampa Bay when he awoke.

Salvatore glanced at Ramello. 'Hey kid,' he said, 'Where do you live?'

Ramello yawned, rubbing his eyes with tiredness. 'It's near Channelside Drive,' he replied. 'Drop me off there, and I'll walk home.'

Officer Jacob looked back, concern etching his features. 'It's getting pretty dark, boy,' he said. 'How far is your home from there?'

'It's near Pizza Hut in West Hillsborough Avenue,' Ramello responded.

'I'll drop him off near Channelside Drive,' Salvatore declared. 'It won't harm him if he walks down a few streets.'

Officer Jacob's expression remained unsatisfied. 'You know it's dangerous?' he challenged.

'Who says I don't know?' Salvatore shot back, then turned to Ramello. 'How old are you?' he asked, his voice softening.

'Eighteen,' Ramello replied.

Salvatore nodded as he stopped the car on Channelside Drive, 'Jump off then,' he instructed.

Ramello jumped out, his hurried footsteps echoing through the dimly lit streets. After entering the street where his house was, he glanced around; something was odd, and the air was full of tension.

Cop cars were on the roadside, their polished surfaces shining under the streetlights. Their presence sent a shiver down Ramello's spine. And there, nestled amongst them, was a sleek, metallic black SUV. Its occupants couldn't be seen because of its dark, tinted windows.

His gaze darted further down the street, and there he saw RD. RD was in handcuffs, and his face was twisted with anger. He was like a coiled spring, ready to unleash violence on anyone who dared to cross his path.

Before Ramello could react, someone grabbed his hair, a painful yank pulling him backwards. He caught his breath and spun around to see Richmond standing there, glaring viciously, and then, with a quick movement, he clamped his hand over Ramello's mouth.

Richmond's grip tightened as he dragged Ramello into a dark alley, its shadows swallowing them whole. Waiting there, like a hungry spider in its web, was Jaylon.

Jaylon glanced at Ramello, 'Why have you brought this guy here?' he asked Richmond.

'He's the weirdo who we're after, you thicko,' Richmond snapped. 'And, Jay, have you called our backup?'

'Yeah, I have,' Jaylon replied. 'But they're taking the mick, and the situation is escalating.'

'RD is getting arrested,' Richmond shouted, 'and they're taking ages to come. Phone them again and tell them to come quickly.'

Jaylon's call connected, and a distant voice crackled through the line. 'What do you want?' the person demanded.

'The police have RD in the police car,' Jaylon shouted. 'You lot are taking the piss!'

The response was a mix of urgency and annoyance: 'We're just a few streets away!' the backup bellowed, 'How fast do you think we are?'

Jaylon slammed the phone down, eyes locking with Richmond's. 'Satisfied?' he asked the question in a challenging way.

'No, I'm not satisfied. I need them to come now!' Richmond shouted with uncontrollable anger.

Suddenly, the roar of a car engine sliced through the quiet alley, shattering the night's stillness. The sound reverberated off the narrow walls, jolting everyone present. Jaylon's curiosity was piqued as he strode towards the end of the alley, peering into the darkness beyond. His eyes widened as he took in the scene which unfolded before him.

Ten shadowy figures emerged from a big, bright red car, spilling out like a swarm of angry hornets. Their movements were swift and aggressive, menace radiating from each man. Jaylon's amusement bubbled forth, a nervous laugh escaping his lips. 'Well,' he quipped, 'I suppose they all crammed themselves into that vehicle. Impressive.'

But Richmond wasn't amused; he yanked Ramello towards the alley's mouth, who was struggling against his iron grip. The air crackled with tension as Richmond punched Ramello's head, a sharp blow that silenced any struggle. Blood trickled down Ramello's temple, but his eyes remained fixed on the unfolding drama, ignoring the pain that surged through his head.

Richmond assessed the situation from the alley, his face contorted with rage. 'Forget their clown car antics,' he snarled, his voice low and evil, 'RD's already in the police car!'

'Calm down, Richie,' Jaylon said in a smooth voice, 'What has he done for you that you want to shield him from prison's cold embrace? Honestly, I want him behind bars and destroyed.'

Richmond glared at him, 'Don't talk rubbish before I silence you with a bullet,' he said through clenched teeth.

'Richie!' Jaylon shouted, yanking him back as a bullet just missed his head, 'Use that thick skull of yours; stay behind and take some cover.'

'Listen, Jay,' Richmond murmured, his voice sounding very dangerous, 'Salvatore's car just pulled up.'

Jaylon's sarcasm flared, 'And what?' he challenged, igniting Richmond's fury.

Richmond's rage erupted like a volcano, 'You know what,' he shouted, 'We need to get rid of Salvatore.'

Jaylon's mockery cut deeper. 'So, we stroll out like Charlie's and get shot at?' he quipped. 'It's o'right; I'm staying put.'

Richmond started losing his patience. 'Shut your gob, Jay!' he roared, creating waves of echoes within the alley.

'Rich...Richie,' Jaylon's voice quivered, his gaze locked on a dark shadow lurking behind Richmond. Fear etched across his face; he yelled furiously, 'Look back, and you'll see your target is right behind ya!'

Richmond spun around, with Ramello still in his grasp, anger running through his veins; he was going to shout for help, but it was too late; Salvatore had already emerged; his gun, cold and unforgiving, he aimed at Richmond's leg.

The gunshot echoed as the bullet tore through his flesh. Richmond fell to the ground, dragging Ramello down with him; blood slowly started to gush out of the wound. Ramello quickly stood up as Richmond released his grip.

Richmond screamed in absolute agony, trying to compress the bleeding, but it seemed like the alley floor was drinking Richmond's blood, the crimson stains seeping into the cracks.

Jaylon's scream shattered the night as terror gripped him. Salvatore's eyes, void of mercy, held Jaylon's gaze.

As Richmond's leg continued to bleed, Jaylon's world tilted. Choices, consequences, and the scent of blood hung heavy.

Salvatore ran over to Ramello, gripping his wrist, 'Come on, kid,' he said, 'Let's get out of here.'

They both ran out of the alley into the open road where violence was brewing like a storm.

'Hide behind that car and stay low,' Salvatore shouted at Ramello, pointing at a nearby police car.

Ramello darted behind the car, his heart beating fast. He could hear the noise of bullets all around him. Suddenly, he saw Salvatore running towards him, who then threw his body on top of him, flattening him to the ground as bullets flew over their heads.

'You're such a stupid boy,' Salvatore snarled, 'I told you to hide behind the car and keep low; why were you bobbing your head up and down? You nearly got killed.'

Ramello swallowed hard; he felt worried; wherever he looked, it was pure bloodshed.

Salvatore stood up, readying himself to fight off the men approaching them. Ramello quickly looked back as he heard footsteps behind him. Standing there was a man with amber eyes and an evil grin. 'Hello, Ramello,' he taunted, whispering his name with hatred.

Ramello realised with terror sinking in his heart that it was RD.

'Why the change in eye colour?' Ramello asked, trying to stall him till Salvatore returned.

'Natural, you oddball,' RD mockingly laughed.

'And how did you get out of the police car?' Ramello asked.

'My crew's got ma back,' RD boasted, seizing Ramello's arm and dragging him towards the big, red car, its paint mirroring the blood-soaked ground.

'No, you don't!' someone's voice came from behind.

RD spun around and received a Roundhouse kick, followed by a Tornado kick in his face from Salvatore, sending the villain sprawling. His nose started to bleed, and his head began to spin from the brutal kicks Salvatore delivered.

Salvatore's gaze bore into Ramello, 'Go, boy, quickly run home,' he rasped.

Ramello turned around and sprinted down the street. Suddenly, three men appeared. He skidded to a halt and looked at the men fearfully.

'Who are you?' one of the men commanded, tilting his head like a curious predator.

'Some kind of...beggar?' the other one sneered, narrowing his green eyes. He started scrutinising Ramello as if he was trying to solve a puzzle.

'He looks like he has never been fed before; that's why he looks like some kind of scrawny chicken,' the last man taunted; he got hold of Ramello's collar, lifting him like a rag doll, 'Who are you?'

Ramello's voice quivered, 'I'm...Ramello.'

'Ramello,' the man repeated, 'Oh! So, you're the one everyone's been trying to find.'

Ramello tried to move away from him, but the man slammed his head into a wall, causing him to lose consciousness.

Chapter 4
Echoes Of An Intruder

Ramello's eyes fluttered open. Sitting near him was Salvatore, looking at him worriedly. 'Are you all right?' he inquired, his face looking sad.

Ramello touched his throbbing head, 'My head hurts,' he admitted.

'I found you at the bottom of the street, near a wall,' Salvatore said, rubbing Ramello's head, 'And you've got a mountain growing on your head.'

'Where am I?' Ramello asked, looking around with bewilderment and staring disapprovingly at the unfamiliar bed he was lying in. The room's opulence and grandeur only deepened his sense of disorientation.

'You're in my house,' Salvatore replied. Standing up, he crossed the room and drew open the curtains, flooding the room with radiant sunlight.

'How long have I been out for?' Ramello asked, staring outside at the morning sun.

'You've been knocked out for the entire night,' Salvatore responded, walking towards him and comfortably sitting at the end of the bed.

'Can you take me home?' Ramello implored.

Salvatore's smile was warm, but there was an odd hesitation in his response. 'Of course, Ramel... lad,' he said, the words trailing off.

Suspicion began to gnaw at Ramello. 'Do you know my name?' he probed, his voice filled with a mix of curiosity and unease.

Salvatore chuckled nervously, rubbing the back of his head. 'No, I didn't quite catch your name,' his eyes met Ramello's, a flicker of uncertainty in them. 'Anyway, what is your name?'

'The name is Ramello,' he replied. Staring hard, he curiously studied Salvatore's peculiar features. The man's face seemed to shift as if it couldn't decide on a single expression.

'Ah, Ramello!' Salvatore mused, his smile lopsided. 'A nice and unique name indeed!'

'OK, so can you take me home?' Ramello asked again.

'Yes, let's go downstairs; I left your trainers there,' Salvatore said, his voice still shaky, betraying his hidden anxiety.

Ramello followed him down the stairs. To his surprise, he found himself in a grand hall, which felt warm from the glow of the morning sun that streamed through the tall, polished glass windows.

'Your house is so dope!' Ramello said, looking around in awe. He put on his trainers and followed Salvatore out of the front door and into his car.

Salvatore's vintage car glided through the streets. Ramello sat comfortably in the passenger seat, his mind a whirlwind of questions and half-formed memories.

The car came to a sudden stop. 'OK, kid, we're here,' Salvatore's voice broke the silence, 'I'll keep in touch; you stay safe now.'

Ramello momentarily hesitated, his heart pounding in his chest, his thoughts racing with fear overwhelming him. He then exited the car and waved Salvatore off, who merely nodded and drove away.

Ramello walked towards his house and knocked on the front door. Frederick swung the door open and enveloped Ramello in a hug, the kind he'd never received from his stoic older brother. 'Ramello! What's going on? Where have you been?' Frederick's voice held a mix of relief and worry.

'Long story, bro,' Ramello said with relief. 'So much crazy shit you won't believe.'

Ramello stepped inside, the familiar scent of home wrapping around him like a warm blanket; he walked into the living room, the fireplace crackling, the sofas inviting. Phillip and Edmond were seated, their expressions a blend of concern and curiosity.

After Ramello told them his story, Phillip sighed and stood up, saying, 'Come on, Edmond and Frederick, let's go to Pizza Hut. His story is making my head hurt.'

'Yeah,' Frederick chimed in, 'He's probably just making up a tone of bullshit and putting us all to sleep, let's get out of here.'

They Left Ramello out as he watched sadly at his brothers leaving the room, their footsteps echoing in the empty space. They totally ignored him, although Edmond did give him the side-eye. He stayed slumped on the sofa, the soft fabric comforting against his back. He stared at the ceiling, his eyes welling with tears.

He had been sitting there for a while when he heard a strange noise. At first, he thought it was his brothers coming back, but the noise was like someone trying to get into the house.

Ramello stood up as fear engulfed him. He sought refuge beneath the living room table, crouching beneath its cloth cover. He stayed still as he heard the door being kicked down.

By the sound of the heavy footsteps, Ramello believed that there were a few men.

'Find that rascal before I rearrange your faces,' shouted a familiar voice.

Ramello sneakily peered out from under the tablecloth and realised it was, in fact, RD; he could feel the sweat dripping down his forehead.

However, RD seemed at ease. He sat sprawled on one of the sofas as if he owned the place, his red contact lenses, which Ramello hated, adding an eerie touch to his face. His joeys fanned out, searching every nook and cranny, their eyes scanning for what seemed to be Ramello himself.

A few moments passed, and one of the men walked back into the living room. 'I can't find the little rat! Are you sure he's even here?' he asked.

'Keep looking, Jaylon,' RD grunted, pulling a lighter from his jeans pocket and lighting a cigarette. 'Homeboy didn't leave the house; it was only his stupid brothers.'

Jaylon nodded like a puppet attached to invisible strings and then retreated.

For an extended period, RD remained seated, taking long, heavy drags, before his two men returned, 'We looked everywhere, we just can't find him!' the other man shouted, angrily throwing his arms up.

RD's eyes narrowed, a cloud of smoke exiting his mouth, 'Let's spread out and check the streets,' he said, marching out of the room.

Ramello's heart pounded as he heard RD's footsteps fade away. He took three sturdy breaths to steady himself and then strained to listen for any noise but heard none. When he was sure RD and his men had gone, he slowly crawled out of his hiding spot. He looked around the room and saw muddy footprints on the plush, cream carpet, and half a cig was left on the sofa. He grimaced at the sight; throwing the cig off, he collapsed onto the couch. He was lazily stretching his arms when the room door was suddenly flung open, and RD barged in.

Ramello looked at him innocently, his heart racing. 'Hi,' he said in a shaky voice, his mind racing with fear as he tried to calculate how to escape from this nightmare that wouldn't end.

RD smirked and walked up to Ramello, his tall, imposing figure casting a shadow over him. He grabbed Ramello by the collar, his grip tight, and stared into his eyes.

'Yo, where have you been? Sneakin' around like we're playin' hide-and-seek,' RD laughed mockingly.

Jaylon and the other man walked into the room, their heavy footsteps echoing in the silence, 'Where did you find him, Devil?' Jaylon asked, his voice filled with a mix of curiosity and suspicion.

'I rolled up back into the room, and there he was, like some ninja with a PhD in invisibility,' RD said, smiling with achievement as he stared into Ramello's worried eyes. 'You got two choices, boy. Come with me, or...' He cracked his knuckles, the sound echoing like a gunshot. 'Well, let's just say the streets ain't gonna be kind to ya.'

'I'm not coming with you!' Ramello screamed, 'Why won't you just back off from me? I'm no use to you.'

RD pulled chewing gum from his pocket and popped it into his mouth. 'You don't wanna come with me, eh?' he sighed. 'Well, I ain't givin' ya a choice.'

Ramello remained standing, staring into RD's bright red eyes, trying to act brave, but he had to keep looking away; the man looked evil.

RD laughed, 'Ya gonna come with me on a nice cruise in ma Lambo.'

Ramello stared at him blankly, but RD didn't give him a choice and shoved him out of the house.

They walked down the street towards a polished red Lamborghini Aventador with dark-tinted windows.

RD opened the passenger door and practically threw Ramello in, 'Belt up, boy,' he said, slamming the door shut.

Ramello silently buckled his seat belt and watched as Jaylon and the other man jumped into another car while RD got into the Lamborghini. He didn't understand why RD had gotten rid of him before; now, he wanted him again.

RD didn't put his seat belt on and started to drive. He drove for a while till they ended up on a motorway.

'Where are you taking me?' Ramello asked tremblingly, remembering that the motorway was the same one Richmond and Jaylon had previously taken him on to meet RD. He clenched his teeth, the bitter taste of lifetime betrayal still on his tongue.

RD's gaze remained fixed on the horizon, the landscape blurring past. His jet-black hair fell across his forehead, 'Wherever I wanna take ya,' he finally replied, his voice smooth as the Lamborghini continued its smooth cruise.

With frustration, Ramello hit his hands against the leather seat, 'I hate your ridiculous remarks!' he shouted, but RD remained calm and still.

RD veered off the motorway, steering the slick car into a skyscraper's parking lot. He parked in one of the bays and jumped out, urgency in every movement. He opened Ramello's door, but Ramello crossed his arms and ignored him.

RD grabbed Ramello's arm and dragged him out, making him stumble.

'That hurt, you devil!' Ramello's cry echoed in the air.

But RD chuckled, his eyes glinting with amusement, 'If ya thought the term 'devil' got me annoyed, nah fam,' he laughed, making his devilish teeth show, 'I vibe with that word.'

Ramello staggered and followed RD into the skyscraper. The skyscraper was luxurious; it had everything an ordinary person would want. RD moved like a predator, his every step commanding attention. Men in tailored suits and women with sharp gazes occupied the building. They moved away like waves before him. Fear etched their expressions, a silent acknowledgement of RD's power. He was no ordinary man; he was a force to be reckoned with.

Ramello kept firing all sorts of questions, but RD ignored him the whole way.

They walked into a glass-made lift. RD pressed number fourteen, and the lift started to move upwards.

'What is this place?' Ramello asked, 'It doesn't look like a hotel; it looks more like an office building.'

RD glared at him, 'Zip it, boy!' he shouted.

Hatred flared within Ramello, but he kept his tongue under control.

As the lift doors opened, they stepped out into a softly lit corridor. The corridors were lined with muted lights, casting a gentle glow. Above them, exquisite chandeliers dangled from the high ceilings, their crystal prisms refracting the light. RD approached a nearby door and withdrew a card from his pocket. With a deliberate swipe against the reader, the lock released, and the door swung open.

RD looked at Ramello. 'Get in, boy,' he snapped, pushing Ramello. They both entered a lavishly decorated room, the door automatically locking behind them.

'Sit on that chair,' RD's command was stern.

Ramello went to sit on the chair RD was pointing at. He looked around; it was indeed an office. He watched RD settle on a more comfortable chair in front of an office desk with a slick desktop computer resting on top of it, his fingers steadily tapping the keyboard. Time had passed, boredom overcame Ramello, and he fell asleep.

RD spat the chewing gum into a bin which he had been chewing on for a long time. He looked up at Ramello, who was fast asleep. 'Wake up, you lazy boy,' he said as he stood and crossed the room to another desk, 'Don't ya understand that it's a matter of life and death for you? Tell me where your dad is!'

Ramello rubbed his eyes, 'What did you just say?' he quietly murmured, still half asleep.

RD smiled cruelly as he opened one of the drawers and retrieved a well-polished pistol. He approached Ramello, placing the gun in his hands, 'Scrutinise this, boy,' he murmured, 'And let it sink in; this gun here is gonna close the final chapter of your story.'

Ramello's hands trembled as he looked at the pistol, which weighed heavy in his hands.

RD studied his reflection in a nearby mirror, brushing his fringe away from his face, which swept low over his forehead, 'Yo, remember,' he said, his eyes fixed on his reflection, 'If ya try to shoot the pistol, you'll be put to shame, cause that joint's got no ammo,'

Chapter 5
The Beckoning Abyss

Ramello observed in silence as RD took his time combing his hair back. He then walked arrogantly to his office desk, holding his phone and dialling a number he knew by heart.

After he rang the number for the hundredth time, somebody answered.

'Sup, Salvatore! How's life treating ya?' RD said, giving out an eerie laugh.

'Now, why would I tell you how I'm feeling?' Salvatore's shout reverberated through the phone.

RD started to swear at Salvatore. Salvatore, no stranger to conflict, threw all the swears back in RD's face.

'Do ya even know why I called, ya dog?' RD thundered, getting bored of abusing Salvatore.

'No, I don't, shithead!' Salvatore screamed, his frustration boiling over.

'Yo, ya hollered so loud that I had to move the phone away from ma ear!' RD shot back.

'You're barking so loud that I wasn't sure if a dog was talking to me from the other end,' Salvatore retorted.

'Anyway, I thought I'd hit up 'cause I've got your boy, Ramello. I gave him ma pistol, something to look at before I shoot him dead,' RD laughed hysterically.

There was silence on the other side, then Salvatore shouted, 'I'm coming right now, and you better let him go, or I'll make you pay dearly.'

RD laughed, 'Ya ain't got a clue where I am.'

'I'll find you,' Salvatore vowed, 'You can run, but you can't hide.'

'Oh really! Come on then, bring it on and bring all your back up as well; we'll see how far ya get,' RD taunted smoothly.

Salvatore slammed the phone down, a reaction which pleased RD; he had never put a phone down himself on anybody in anger.

RD turned and faced to Ramello, 'Ha! What dya think about that then?' he asked, walking towards him.

Ramello stared at him, 'I have no interest in you and what you do!' he replied, clenching his teeth.

RD tapped Ramello's back and delivered a chilling message: 'Enjoy these remaining precious moments of your pathetic life before I end it.' He then strode swiftly over to the balcony's glass doors and slid them open. He walked onto the balcony and enjoyed the fresh air blowing on his face. He looked towards the south, where the city sprawled, a mosaic of glass and steel. Other skyscrapers punctuate the skyline, each with its own story.

Ramello looked at him, his eyes blazing with hatred. He glanced at the gun, wishing it had a bullet inside it. He stood up and crept silently towards RD. Hoping to catch him off guard, he kicked RD in the shin with a well-practised move. RD looked back at him with a confused face, 'Huh! Were ya tryna hurt me? I didn't even feel a thing, but I guess you might have bruised your foot,' he said with a chuckle.

Ramello's face turned bright red, 'No, I was just...just...umm, I was just...,' lost for words, Ramello froze.

'I wouldn't recommend ya do anything stupid like that again. I will kill ya, and I'll enjoy every bit of it,' RD replied, his voice low and measured, 'Don't try to change my mind with your foolish acts.'

Ramello felt annoyed; he couldn't let RD's threat go unanswered, 'I actually meant to do that because you're evil, and I hate you,' he blurted out.

'That's even more sour,' RD chuckled, a hint of amusement tugging at the corners of his lips, 'Listen, ya little shit, ya think you can harm me? You're nothin' but a fish in water. Look at ya!'

'Just let me go!' Ramello shouted.

'You're such a typical child,' RD smirked, 'You remind me of ma son.'

'Your son? Who's that?' Ramello demanded.

RD side-eyed him, 'Yo, kid, can't be tellin' ya everything now, can I?' he replied.

'Can you stop calling me a kid? I'm eighteen! I'm a grown man!' Ramello shouted.

'Oh Really!' RD's eyebrows shot up, 'I never knew that. I thought you were about two,' he mocked, 'You're a real toddler, ain't ya?'

'You truly are the devil!' Ramello screamed.

'Ah! Your words hurt so much, like daggers piercing through ma body,' RD said sarcastically. He gripped Ramello's arm and whispered in his ear, 'Do you know what I wanna do with ya? I've decided I don't really wanna shoot ya anymore; that would be too mundane, no fun in that,' a twisted smile curved his lips, 'I wanna throw you off the balcony instead,' he mocked.

Ramello staggered back, fear sweeping through his body and tears filled his eyes, 'Just leave me alone,' he pleaded desperately.

'Your tears are softenin' my heart,' RD said with sarcasm in his voice. 'Got me feelin' all mushy inside.'

Ramello stormed into the room and sat back on the chair; he didn't know what to do; there was no choice but to get shot or thrown off the balcony, 'Can't you just shoot me dead? If that's what you want to do with me, instead of biding time,' he shouted.

RD turned around and smiled at him, 'You don't worry about me killin' ya, I can do it whenever I want, even when you're asleep,' he laughed, 'But remember, boy, I'm going to make sure you're starin' down the barrel of ma gun before I shoot you.'

Ramello looked into his eyes, 'I don't care when or how you kill me,' he shouted. 'JUST DO IT!'

RD started ignoring him and went over to his desk.

Suddenly, there was a loud knock on the door; RD sighed and stood up, his movements deliberate, like a predator sensing its prey. He crossed the room and swung the door open. 'What do you want?' he asked, his voice a low growl.

The twenty-two-year-old visitor stood there, his hazel eyes wide with curiosity, 'I came to see what you were doing,' he casually replied.

RD ushered him in, locking the door behind him.

'Who's this?' the man asked, glancing at Ramello, who sat nearby, fidgeting with his hands.

'He's the guest I was talkin' about, Hershy,' RD replied, comfortably sitting in a chair.

Hershy looked at Ramello, 'I was expecting him to be about thirty,' he said in a confused tone, 'He looks like a kid.'

'The gangster is barely thirty-five, and you believe Ramello is thirty years of age,' RD scoffed, rolling his eyes.

'That's how you explained him to me,' Hershy retorted, sitting near RD. 'So, what's your next plan?'

RD's gaze shifted to Ramello, which started making him squirm, 'My next plan,' he said, lowering his voice, 'Is to get rid of his dirty spawn.'

Hershy smiled. 'I've got something planned too!'

'What?' RD asked, his eyes narrowing.

'I'm going to bury you six feet under,' Hershy laughed seriously, rising from his chair quickly. 'We'll see who gets killed.'

RD looked at him as if he didn't hear him, 'Do you know what, Hershy,' he said, sliding his hand under his jumper, his fingers brushing against cold steel, 'I'm gonna shoot you dead, you backstabber.'

Hershy laughed, 'We will see about that,' he said.

'Yeah, we will,' RD said; his movements were swift as he drew a handgun from his belt holster. The shot rang out, and Hershy fell to the floor, clutching his leg. Blood seeped into the carpet, staining it dark red.

With anger, RD walked over to Ramello, 'Your life was meant to be a bit longer,' he roared, his finger on the trigger, 'But since this guy came...' the gunshot echoed, and Ramello's scream pierced the room as the bullet struck his arm, but RD wasn't bothered, doing bad things made him happy.

'Now try backstabbing me,' RD laughed, settling back into his chair. He watched both men, screaming with pain, with cruel satisfaction.

A repeated knock on the door interrupted the commotion. RD went to see who it was, 'My lovely Ander!' he said as he opened the door.

Ander walked in, his smile fading as he saw the blood-smeared scene before him. 'Dad, what's going on? Why is it like a blood bath here?' he asked.

'That's because Hershy tried to backstab me, and that one over there...' RD gestured towards Ramello, who lay on the floor, eyes wide with pain, 'You know about that one anyway.'

'Is that actually him?' Ander asked in surprise, walking over to Ramello, and kicking him in the side, making him scream with pain.

'Yeah, that's him, Ander,' RD said, 'Now can you get the kettle singin' and brew up a cuppa for me, boyo?'

'Yep, Dad,' Ander said. He put the kettle on to boil, made the coffee, and gave it to RD, who started enjoying the warmth of the mug on his palm.

RD started to sip, making a dreadful slurping noise; he continued scrutinising Hershy and Ramello.

Ander sat near him, 'What are you going to do with these two?' he asked, eyes gleaming.

'Toss 'em in the trash, innit? Ain't no other place for 'em; they're no use for me,' RD retorted with a sarcastic laugh.

'That's where losers belong,' Ander laughed loudly.

Both RD and Ander enjoyed a moment of amusement as they scorned Hershy and Ramello.

RD looked at Ander, 'Listen, homie, you just stay here,' he said, 'I gotta handle some important business.'

Ander nodded and watched as his dad walked out of the room. He stood and walked over to Ramello, 'Get up,' he ordered.

Ramello looked at him suspiciously. His arm was wounded from the gunshot, yet this stranger wanted him on his feet. 'Get away from me!' he shouted.

Ander looked at him and sighed; he grabbed Ramello's wounded arm, trying to make him stand up.

'You idiot!' Ramello shouted, 'Why are you grabbing my wounded arm?' He clutched his arm with pain, which had immensely increased. The blood stained his hand.

'Sorry,' Ander murmured. He was just about to tell him something when the door swung open, and RD strode in. 'What dya think you're doin'?' RD asked suspiciously when he saw Ander standing near Ramello.

'I was just kicking the living daylights out of him,' Ander lied, his voice steady; it seemed like he was speaking the truth because Ramello was crying, but Ramello knew he lied, but why?

RD relaxed in his chair, pulled several papers out of a drawer, and started writing on them.

Ander made Ramello sit back down and sat near his dad, 'Dad,' he whispered.

Suddenly, RD's mood changed; his eyes, once warm, now bore into Ander like shards of ice, 'Shut up, Ander! I don't want to hear from ya,' he spat, venom dripping from his lips, picking his gun off the desk, 'Get out of ma face before I gun ya down.'

Ander's mouth fell open, 'Are you talking to me this way, Dad?' he asked, 'You've never threatened me like this before.'

RD, the one who had once cradled Ander's dreams, shouted, 'Don't answer me back,' he said, cocking the pistol with practised ease.

Ander stood up and pulled a pocketknife out of his jeans pocket, 'I'm not going to let you shoot me,' he shouted and then lunged forward with the knife tightly held in his hand. It pierced RD's flesh, and blood flowed, staining their shared history.

RD stood up, put his hand on his arm and then removed it; it was covered with blood.

'You're a dead man, Ander,' he declared, and then a gunshot shattered the room.

Ander fell to the ground, his leg burning with pain, and blood started gathering beneath him.

RD laughed an evil laugh, then viciously banged the back of his gun into Ander's head, making his world spin, which left him unconscious.

Chapter 6
Escape From The Red Devil

RD paced up and down the room, looking at his victims.

'Ander, Ander, Ander,' he repeated in disappointment, 'How'd it feel? That's what happens when ya don't follow ma instructions; I've told ya repeatedly not to have a soft spot for Ramello. That's why you've ended up with a bullet in yer leg, and the next one is gonna be between yer eyes. Just look at Hershy; that's what ya get for being disobedient,' he laughed.

Ander looked at him but didn't answer him.

RD looked at his arm again, his hand covered in blood from holding the stab wound; it was still bleeding a lot.

He furiously looked back at Ander, 'I reckon I'm fixin' to put an end to yer days,' he confessed.

'End it then,' Ander shouted, 'I don't care anymore.'

RD grabbed his gun and pointed it at Ander, 'Dare me, and I'll pop ya,' he taunted, aiming the barrel at Ander's chest.

'Shoot me,' Ander shouted again, tears rolling down his cheeks, 'I know I went against what you said, but there was no need to do what you did; you could have spoken nicely to me.'

RD's laughter echoed around the room, devoid of mercy, 'Why waste words on you, fool?' he sneered. 'You're just another Hershy, defying the boss's orders.' RD stepped closer, pressing the gun's cold metal against Ander's temple. 'Forget boss,' he whispered, 'I'm your dad as well.'

A blaring car horn sliced through the room. RD's gaze scanned the area surrounding the balcony; he walked towards it, his eyes unblinking, 'Salvatore,' he muttered, the name a curse on his lips.

A black SUV came to a screeching stop in the car park below, followed by a line of identical beasts.

RD's pulse quickened; this was no ordinary arrival. He turned around and stormed back inside the room. His pistol, cold and unforgiving, was held tightly in his hand. Ramello, wide-eyed and trembling, watched as RD pelted it out of the room.

He lay there briefly, listening to the racket outside the room. Suddenly, the door flung open, and Salvatore came running in. 'Hey lad! Come on, let's go,' he bellowed. He grabbed Ramello's injured arm, making him scream in pain.

'Sorry, lad,' Salvatore apologised grimly, seeing the blood on his arm, 'We'll get you fixed up pretty soon.'

He gently made Ramello stand up, quickly looking around the room. His eyes acknowledged the presence of Hershy and Ander sprawled on the floor. 'We need to get out of here fast,' he said as he hurried out of the room.

They started running down the corridor. Ramello tried to keep up with Salvatore, but Salvatore was running too fast.

'Come on, kid, we're nearly there; keep going,' Salvatore urged, slowing his pace, 'You can't take long; RD is going to catch up to us.'

They ran around a bend. Just then, they saw RD running towards them. Salvatore quickly pulled his gun out. They both started to fire bullets at each other.

Salvatore shot three bullets, and all of them missed except for one, which hit RD in the leg; he crashed to the ground and screamed in pain.

Salvatore grabbed Ramello's hand, and they both started to run.

They ran into a lift, and Salvatore hit the ground floor button. The lift descended smoothly, stopping at the ground floor. Its doors slowly opened. As he observed with precaution, Salvatore was alert and quickly entered the lobby.

'This way!' Salvatore shouted, pulling Ramello towards him as a bullet flew past their heads; they could see one of RD's joeys getting closer.

Salvatore's aim was on target as he shot bullets at the man, hitting him in the head and chest, killing him on the spot.

'Come on, we can't waste time around here,' Salvatore said, panting. Ramello's eyes were fixed on the man; he'd never seen something so horrible before, and the blood on the floor made him dizzy; he thought the horror movies his brother Frederick watched were gory.

They exited the skyscraper and headed for Salvatore's car, parked in front, 'Jump in my car,' Salvatore shouted, but Ramello was still in shock.

Lightheaded, Ramello flung himself into the car, slamming the door shut. Salvatore hurriedly got into the driver's seat and started revving the engine impatiently. He snatched his phone from the dashboard and began to ring someone, 'Officer Jacob,' he panted as the person answered. 'Where are you?'

'I'm relaxing in my house, having a nice mug of mocha,' Officer Jacob replied calmly.

'You weirdo,' Salvatore's voice erupted, 'We've run into a problem at 200 South Orange on S County Road, and you're sipping mocha!' he shouted, 'Is your skull cracked? Does it need servicing?'

'I didn't know shit was going on; nobody told me,' Officer Jacob said, his confusion evident.

'Well, get your lazy ass off your comfortable sofa and get down here right now!' Salvatore screamed in anger.

'I'm on my way,' Officer Jacob said, slamming the phone down.

Salvatore increased the speed of his car. 'Hold on tight, kid,' he said as he swerved around a car and sped through red lights.

Ramello had never experienced such crazy driving before, but they were in a serious situation, and he didn't want to disturb Salvatore because he knew he would get annoyed.

They sped through never-ending streets until they arrived at a cramped cul-de-sac.

Salvatore jumped out and opened Ramello's door, 'Quickly get out, boy,' he said hurriedly, 'I need to hide you before we get spotted.'

Salvatore tightened his grip on Ramello's hand as he led him to a run-down house. He knocked on the door, and after a brief wait, a middle-aged man opened it.

'Hi, Salvatore,' the man greeted him, smiling warmly, 'It's been a while since I've heard from you.'

'It has been a while, but I really need you to help right now; I need you to hide this boy in your house,' Salvatore replied.

'Of course,' the man chirped happily, stepping aside, 'Come in.'

Salvatore pushed Ramello into the house and then darted back to his car.

'What's your name?' the man asked, locking the door behind him.

'Ramello,' he replied, smiling nervously.

'That name reminds me of someone,' the man mused, his eyes flickering with recognition, 'Anyway, come into the living room and what happened to your arm?'

'I was shot,' Ramello murmured, the words fading with weakness from the ordeal.

'That had to hurt,' the man said, pity in his eyes, 'Come here, boy, and I'll clean the wound and bandage it.'

The man led Ramello into a small room; its tight space made him feel suffocated. He cleaned and bandaged Ramello's arm, 'I'll get you a warm drink; that will help,' he said, walking out of the room.

After a bit, the man returned with some tea, 'Here you go, boy,' the man said kindly, 'You stay in my house; I need to go outside because I have to tend to something; I'll be back.'

Ramello nodded, 'OK, I'll stay here.'

'Good,' the man said, then left the room quietly.

Lonely and scared, Ramello sank into the warm sofa and started sipping the tea. His eyes moved quickly around the room, searching for any signs of who the man was.

It was getting late, and a storm was approaching. It gathered strength quickly as lightning slashed across the sky, illuminating the room in eerie flashes. Shadows danced on the walls, whispering secrets as thunder rumbled a primal warning. Ramello was getting fidgety and bored, wondering why the man hadn't returned yet.

Minutes stretched into hours, and the man still hadn't returned.

Ramello, feeling a sudden urge, walked out of the room and put on his shoes. He found the house key hanging on a nail near the door.

He opened the door and stepped out into the night, the rain clinging to his skin like icy fingers. He turned, locked the door behind him, posted the key through the letterbox, and started walking down the street.

He flicked the hood of his jumper onto his head and wrapped his arms tightly around his waist. The wind was howling, and the rain painfully whipped his face. His left arm throbbed, an unbearable ache from the gunshot wound, making any simple movement a struggle, but determination propelled him forward.

He started walking around the corner of the street, casually observing his surroundings. The streets were quiet and dark; the only thing that showed him the way was the moon's shining light, which seemed to peek through the stormy clouds. Its glow painted the cobblestone silver, revealing puddles of water that mirrored the sky.

He looked up at the sky and let the rain hit his face. Suddenly, he heard footsteps behind him. He spun around, his heart lodged in his throat. A figure emerged from the shadows, tall and cloaked in black, with electric green eyes piercing the darkness.

Ramello backed off, 'Who are you?' he asked, but he noticed that this man had different-coloured eyes.

The stranger chuckled, a sound that echoed off the wet walls. His voice was like a blade slicing through the rain. 'It's VD.'

'I don't know you,' Ramello stammered, his heart pounding.

The man flicked his hood off, revealing features that mirrored RD's but were darker and more dangerous. His ebony-black hair flowed over his forehead with dyed silver streaks intertwined with the black hair, like threads of moonlight woven into the night. Around his neck, he wore a silver chain, its design mysterious and captivating. His features held a dangerous allure, a blend of ruggedness and refinement. His chiselled jawline framed a mouth that could both charm and intimidate. His green eyes bore into Ramello's, seeming to leave an indelible mark. The silver streaks in his hair caught the moonlight, accentuating his handsome, enigmatic appearance. His lips bore a shade of deep crimson, like petals of a forbidden flower, curved into a smile. The air around him seemed to hum with secrets, and as he smiled, it was as if the night itself leaned in to listen. 'It's VD,' he repeated. 'You're in my world now, Ramello.'

His laughter, a rich baritone, echoed through the night, carrying both mirth and a hint of melancholy. As he began to sing, his voice wove a haunting melody—a velvet tenor, each note resonating with secrets and longing. It was as if the very stars leaned in to listen, captivated by the enigma of this man.

'In the darkness, shadows slinking deep,
Fear grasps your soul as secrets you keep.
Look into my eyes, a chilling abyss,
Where nightmares abide, and horrors persist.
Feel your heart cry, a sorrowful wail,
Echoes of horror that will never fail.
Walk by my side on this night so eerie,
Haunted whispers, whispers so dreary.'

Ramello started to feel worried as VD got closer to him and carried on singing:

'Don't try to hide, for I see your fear,
Every tremulous step, every silent tear.
In this twisted world where nightmares roam,

There's nowhere to escape, no safety to find home.
Beware, dear soul, the darkness will embrace,
As you wander lost in this forsaken space.
For in my chilling gaze, a shadow lies,
That consumes all light, and innocence dies.'

VD gave an evil laugh, his eyes gleaming like shards of broken glass, and the silver streaks in his hair reflected the moon's light. In one swift motion, he seized Ramello's shoulders, his grip like iron and slammed him against a wall; the impact stole the breath from his lungs. The air seemed to thicken as VD pulled a gun from his coat, its metal glinting in the dim light. He pressed the muzzle against Ramello's temple, a chilling reminder of his vulnerability.

'Tell me, young man,' VD began sternly, 'Where is your pathetic dad?'

Ramello felt scared. Why was everyone asking him this wretched question? 'I don't know,' he said in a low tone. The gun's pressure against his temple intensified.

A sudden force yanked VD backwards, making him fall to the ground, and he screamed with anger, 'Wherever I am, you're always there!'

The man, who had attacked VD, laughed, 'Because I'm stuck to ya like gum on a hot sidewalk.'

Ramello looked at the man and realised it was nobody other than RD himself.

'Step away from the boy, Violent Devil,' RD's voice thundered. 'Or you're a dead man.'

'Nah, the boys mine,' VD claimed, his words dripping with venom, 'I got the kid first, and I'm gonna wrench the truth from his trembling lips about his insane dad.'

'Shut your gob and get out of here,' RD commanded, retrieving a gun from his waistband, 'This is my turf, and the boy belongs to me.'

Suddenly, RD staggered and collapsed onto the ground, pain etched across his face. 'Who the bloody hell is that?' His cry echoed.

Ramello's gaze shifted, and to his surprise, Salvatore stood behind him with a knife held firmly in his hands. 'It's me, The Brutal Gangster,' he laughed and turned to VD, his knife glinting. 'I haven't seen you for a long time,' he taunted, plunging the blade into VD's arm, causing his gun to slip from his grasp and clatter on the road. The air thickened with tension as VD's scream echoed throughout the neighbourhood.

Salvatore grabbed Ramello, his grip unyielding. 'Why are you out of the house, you stupid boy?' His voice held a blend of concern and fury. Ramello's tongue felt like lead, his mind racing for excuses.

Before Ramello could respond, Salvatore seized his arm, and they fled down the rain-slicked street towards Salvatore's SUV. 'You're going to get yourself killed,' said Salvatore as he opened the back door for Ramello. He whacked the door shut before Ramello could even fully get his legs in. Ramello screamed at the top of his lungs as the door hit his left leg.

'Sorry, boy,' Salvatore said, 'But you're too slow.'

He jumped into the driver's seat, started the car, and sped off.

'How did you know where I was?' Ramello asked.

Salvatore's eyes remained fixed on the road, his knuckles white against the steering wheel, 'You don't worry about that; you just think about how lucky you are that I came when I did,' he replied, 'And if you ever do this again, it's going to be the end of you, and I can't help you if you don't listen.'

Ramello stayed quiet because he knew he was in the wrong. 'Where are you taking me?' he asked curiously, changing the subject, but Salvatore didn't answer.

After a while, Ramello asked, 'Can I ask you something?'

Salvatore sighed, 'You're really talkative, aren't you, kid? And what is it?' he grumbled.

'How come these weird men are after me and keep asking me where my dad is when I don't even know who my dad actually is?' he questioned.

For a moment, Salvatore kept silent, 'Some questions,' he said in a low, vivid tone, 'Are keys to doors we shouldn't open.'

Ramello was going to ask him what he meant when suddenly Salvatore's phone started ringing. He answered, 'Hi, how are you, Under G?' he asked smoothly.

'Fine,' the caller replied, 'How did your mission go?'

Salvatore sighed, 'Good,' he muttered, 'The boy is in my car, and I'm taking him to the police station to get his thick brain serviced. He's really naive, not taking this situation seriously.'

The man on the other end chuckled. 'He is definitely very foolish, and I understand that it makes you feel angry when he doesn't listen,' he agreed.

Ramello couldn't hold back, 'I'm not foolish or naive!' his voice erupted from the back of the car.

Salvatore glanced at him through the main mirror, 'Yes, you are,' he retorted, 'If you weren't, then you would have never left the house in the first place.'

'I can go where I please and go where I want,' Ramello's frustration increased, 'Last week, I was walking around like a normal person, and now I'm getting escorted in big SUVs by these gangsters.'

Salvatore chuckled and continued talking on the phone, 'The boy is throwing a tantrum.'

'Let him; it's understandable. I would find it weird if suddenly people were going after me and men who are a hundred years older than me were taking me to different places I don't know about,' the other man replied.

'I know,' Salvatore sighed with disappointment, steering the car with one hand into a police station car park, 'Guess what?'

'What?' the man asked.

Salvatore switched to a heavily accented voice, which Ramello didn't understand and found annoying.

The man laughed and then spoke back in a heavy accent that couldn't be understood.

'Anyway, I need to go,' Salvatore said.

'No problem,' the man replied, putting the phone down.

Salvatore parked in one of the parking bays, got out of the car and opened the door for Ramello, who jumped out and followed Salvatore into a small office detached from the bustling police station.

They walked into an office with a narrow corridor leading to a room. The room had many desks with computers. At the far end of the room, a man sat deeply engrossed in his work, his fingers moving quickly on his computer's keyboard.

'Hi, Officer Benjamin,' Salvatore said.

Officer Benjamin looked up at him, his eyes weary but sharp, 'You here with the boy?'

Salvatore nodded and nudged Ramello forward.

Chapter 7
The Unknown Phone Call

Officer Benjamin sighed and stood up, 'Good to meet you, lad,' he said, shaking Ramello's hands, 'Take a seat, please.'

Ramello glanced at Salvatore, seeking guidance. Salvatore's nod was a silent command, and Ramello sat down.

'Do you know why you're here?' asked Officer Benjamin, rummaging in a drawer; he sat back down in front of his desk.

Ramello shook his head, 'No, I don't know.'

'I already told you,' Salvatore's laugh cut through the room, 'You're in deep shit and you need to get your brain serviced.'

Ramello scowled, 'What is the actual reason?'

Officer Benjamin leaned back, 'The reason isn't too different from what Salvatore is saying,' he admitted, 'and also to keep you off the streets.'

Ramello's gaze shifted from one man to the other, 'How come you lot can't drop me off at my brother's house?' he challenged.

Salvatore and Officer Benjamin exchanged a glance, an unspoken conversation, then Officer Benjamin turned to Ramello, 'The reason is...it's just to keep you safe.'

Ramello looked at them suspiciously.

'Nothing to worry about, boy,' Salvatore added, patting Ramello's back, 'You'll be safe in here.'

'He's right,' Officer Benjamin said.

'Come on, Ben,' Salvatore said, 'Let's go, but I'm warning you, boy, if you move out of this room, I will mush you into puree.'

Ramello hated Salvatore's attitude but didn't say anything.

The room echoed with the fading footsteps of Salvatore and Officer Benjamin. But then, a spark of defiance ignited within Ramello.

He took his phone out of his trouser pocket. The screen illuminated, and he dialled Edmond's number, desperation clawing at his throat.

'Hi,' Edmond said, his voice groggy and disinterested.

'Where are you, Ed?' Ramello asked.

'Home, where else?' Edmond's reply was casual, 'And where are you?'

Ramello hesitated, then blurted out the truth. 'I'm in Tampa Bay cop station,' he confessed, the words heavy with fear and frustration.

Suddenly laughter, which brought chills down his spine, erupted from the background.

'Who's that?' Ramello demanded, the freaky laughter seemed to freeze his blood, 'It doesn't sound like any of my bro's.'

'Well, it is your bros,' the so-called Edmond chuckled, 'Your bros are in my house, and they are part of me now.'

Ramello's mind raced, 'What does that mean?' he shouted in despair, 'Whoever you are, my brothers will never be bad like you.'

'Bad?' the man laughed, 'I can send you pictures of them, captured, vulnerable, in my house, and now they're going to become part of my crew. They didn't come willingly, you know. I had to put a gun to their heads.'

'Who are you?' Ramello's voice cracked.

'I'm VD,' the reply slithered through the phone.

'You better let them go!' Ramello shouted.

'A little boy thinks I'm going to listen to his ridiculous request,' VD taunted.

Ramello slammed the phone down, the room spun around him, and his tears blurred the room.

'Why is my life so horrid?' he cried out, the weight of his existence crushing him.

He stood up and started pacing up and down the room, his head spinning with tension.

His phone rang, and it was a withheld number. 'Hi,' he said, answering the phone, his voice brittle.

Nobody answered, so he disconnected the phone. He was about to put it in his pocket when the phone rang again.

'Hello,' Ramello said in an annoyed voice.

'Hi, Ramello,' the slurpy voice on the other side made him cringe.

'Who is it?' Ramello whispered.

'Me, who else?' the person replied in the same dirty, slurpy voice.

'OK, Me,' Ramello scoffed, his fear masked by sarcasm, 'I've never known someone named Me.'

Me's laughter echoed, a twisted melody, 'One cheeky boy you are.'

'What do you want, and who are you?' Ramello insisted, his heart pounding.

Me sighed and then let out a dirty laugh, 'I am waiting for you outside the police station, if you want to know who I am, then come on out; we need to talk, and I'll even tell you my actual name.'

'Listen, Me,' Ramello said, trying to act calm and brave, 'I'm not getting out of the police station.'

'Then I'm coming in,' Me's laugh held a hint of madness.

The phone disconnected, leaving Ramello trembling.

After a while, the door opened, and a man walked in, 'Hi, Ramello,' the man's voice oozed from his lips.

'Who in the world are you?' Ramello asked.

'I'm Me, I already told you,' Me laughed again.

'OK, Me,' Ramello's voice quivered, 'So, why are you here, and what do you want from me?'

'I want to...' Me stopped, his eyes glinting, 'I'm here to put you out of your misery, Me's good at kickboxing, you know.'

'How on earth did you get in here, you madman?' Ramello felt uneasy at this abnormal person.

'Did you not know madmen are capable of absolutely anything?' Me said, still talking with the same dirty slurp in his voice like a drunkard.

'What do you want from me?' Ramello yelled, his face turning pale.

Me walked towards him, 'You're a scrawny lad, ain't ya,' he said, observing Ramello up and down.

Ramello studied Me's face and recognised who he was, he was the man who had broken into the house with RD and Jaylon.

Before Ramello could react, Me's foot connected with his face. Ramello staggered back, falling onto the floor, tasting blood in his mouth. His fury surged, and he pushed himself up.

Me was somehow on the other side of the room, looking out of the window, his hair falling into place as if he hadn't even assaulted Ramello. He turned around to face Ramello, 'Ready for another one?' he taunted.

'Shut up,' Ramello spat, 'You've already busted my nose.'

'It should feel like a tickle; it's just a tap!' Me said, sarcasm in his voice. He looked into Ramello's eyes and then lunged at him again.

Ramello screamed but it was too late, Me delivered a front snap kick in his face and then punched him in the lip, making it bleed.

Ramello's sobs echoed through the room.

'Ramello, you're such a baby!' mocked Me, wiping imaginary tears away from his eyes; then suddenly, his attention moved away from Ramello, 'Hi,' he said in a shaky voice, looking towards the door.

VD walked up to him, 'You're RD's lackey, aren't you?' he spat.

'No, no,' Me shook his head, eyes gleaming with menace, 'I'm your slave, you idiot.'

VD looked at him with anger and slapped him across the face.

'Oooh! That really hurt,' Me quipped, rubbing his face mockingly.

Me made VD feel inferior and was embarrassing him.

He looked at Ramello who was still on the floor, sobbing, 'What have you done to the kid's face?' he asked as he lifted Ramello's tear-streaked face.

'He wanted a makeover, so I rearranged his face a little; looks nice, doesn't it?' Me laughed. 'I guess you don't like the way you look either. Don't worry, I'll help you too.'

VD wiped Ramello's tears away and dabbed the blood away from his lip with a tissue. 'Don't worry, boy,' he whispered, helping him stand up.

Me sniggered, 'Acting like his dad, are you? Well, get ready for a family reunion.' Me sent VD sprawling across the room with a flying kick to the face.

VD clutched his nose, which started bleeding heavily, 'You watch, now you've done it,' he snarled.

The door swung open, and Salvatore and Officer Benjamin entered happily, engaged in a conversation. They suddenly screamed simultaneously when they noticed the commotion in the room.

VD quickly scrambled to his feet, behaving like he was the tough one.

'Wherever you are, lad, these lot will always catch up to you,' Salvatore shouted, pulling his gun out of his cross-draw holster.

Briefly, shock overcame Officer Benjamin; he let go of his mug of coffee, making it shatter on the floor.

VD's eyes darted between Salvatore and Me; he couldn't make out whose face to smash up first. He then pulled his gun quickly out and locked eyes with Salvatore. 'Listen, Salvatore,' he hissed. 'You know who I am, so don't try to shoot a bullet. Put your gun down on the floor and step back.'

Salvatore rolled his eyes, his fingers tightening around the trigger of the gun, 'Who says I don't know who you are?' he retorted, ignoring VD's command.

Ramello observed the heated argument between the men, unexpectedly experiencing a peculiar sense of compassion for VD.

Salvatore was just about to press the trigger when Ramello screamed, 'No! don't shoot him!'

Salvatore stared at him strangely. 'Are you all right, lad, or have you gone mental?' he snapped.

VD looked a bit confused as well, and weirdly stared at Ramello, 'What's up, Ramello?' he asked.

'Sticking up for a bloody devil, are you?' Salvatore shouted, 'After how much I've done for you and would even give up my life for you, should I shoot you instead? You ungrateful piece of work!'

'Salvatore,' VD's voice came out like a hissing snake, 'There's always a connection between blood bonds.'

'Shut your fat trap,' Salvatore snapped, clenching his teeth angrily.

Ramello stood mute, shocked at VD's strange statement of blood bonds. Salvatore's finger itched to shoot at VD, but something was stopping him—VD's sudden statement. He also didn't want to get Ramello involved in any danger. 'You still act like a spoilt child who doesn't know what reality is.' Salvatore remarked.

Ramello opened his mouth to say something, but Salvatore moved swiftly and, with one sudden movement, pulled him away from VD, 'Go stand near Officer Benjamin and don't get involved; this is for grown-ups to deal with.'

Ramello quickly went and stood near Officer Benjamin; he knew Salvatore was not going to listen to him about not shooting VD.

Ramello looked at Me, leaning against one of the walls, observing the chaos like an interested spectator at a twisted theatre. His eyes danced with amusement.

Ramello could see Salvatore, who was pointing his gun straight at VD. Then he heard Me snigger; the unsettling noise made everybody in the room feel uneasy.

'You alien, Shut your nasty gob,' Ramello screamed out of anger. 'You're so horrible, Me!'

'Me's not going to shut his perfumed mouth,' Me chuckled.

VD burst into laughter when he saw Salvatore giving Me dirties, 'Why do you call yourself Me?' Salvatore demanded.

'Is that meant to be a pen name?' VD asked.

Me brushed his black hair away from his forehead. 'Indeed,' he replied, 'A pen name crafted especially for Ramello.'

'Why are you not telling us your actual name?' VD asked, 'I mean, I don't know your name myself.'

Me started fidgeting with his hands behind his back, and then suddenly, he drew them forward with a glinting gun held tightly in his grasp, 'Nobody needs to worry about my actual name and also the name Me; just think about what I'm going to do to your precious lives,' he laughed.

VD bore the brunt of Me's wrath as he shot bullets towards VD. They tore through his flesh, leaving crimson trails across the floor. Ramello, torn between loyalty and terror, sprinted towards VD. A sudden pain travelled through his leg as Me's shot found its mark.

Ramello collapsed, his vision blurring. The room spun, reality disappearing. Darkness encroached, swallowing him whole.

Chapter 8
Treacherous Nurse

Ramello's hazel eyes shot open, the hospital room's light almost blinding him. He noticed his leg was bandaged; suddenly, a gentle hand ran through his hair, and he turned to see Salvatore perched on the edge of the bed.

'Hi, lad,' Salvatore's voice was a soothing balm, 'Are you all right?'

Ramello sighed, 'I've got a banging headache. What happened to your face?' he asked, gesturing to a deep cut running across Salvatore's cheek.

'I tried to save your life from Me, and the idiot slashed me with his blade, that's what,' Salvatore replied, wincing as he touched the wound on his face.

Ramello squinted at him, 'You're quite invincible; you seem to be someone who never gets shot,' he said in amazement.

Just then, a nurse entered the room, 'Hi,' she greeted Ramello, 'How is your leg feeling?'

'I don't know,' Ramello answered, 'I can't really feel it.'

'Well, that's the effects of the numbing medication we injected into your leg before the operation,' the nurse responded.

'I don't remember any operation!' Ramello exclaimed.

'You wouldn't have because you've been unconscious for a few days,' the nurse said, studying him, 'The doctor said you look well enough to go home; you're a lucky young man; it could have been worse.'

Ramello nodded with approval, slowly lifting his legs over the edge of the bed and attempting to stand up, but pain ripped through his leg, and he fell to the floor.

Salvatore and the nurse ran towards him. 'Are you all right?' they asked simultaneously, helping him up.

'Does it look like I'm OK?' Ramello snapped, gritting his teeth with pain.

'I don't really think you're ready to go home,' said the nurse.

'No,' Ramello insisted, gripping his leg, 'I'm fine, I'm fine.'

'OK, I guess you're fine,' the nurse said unsurely, making eye contact with Salvatore, who grinned.

'I'll take him home,' Salvatore offered.

'Are you his dad?' asked the nurse.

'No, I'm his un...' Salvatore hesitated then corrected himself, 'I'm just a family friend.'

The nurse looked at him and then laughed, 'Are you really a family friend?'

Salvatore met her gaze, 'And what's the problem? Is that an issue?' he asked.

The nurse walked over to a drawer and opened it. Salvatore quickly grabbed his gun from his shoulder holster, its coldness and weight familiar against his palm, 'You work for RD, don't you? You bloody bitch!' Salvatore asked, cocking his gun.

The nurse laughed, 'Who else do I work for? You daft dog!' she said, then lunged at Salvatore with a knife in her hands.

Salvatore fired a bullet, but it missed. Agony erupted in his side as the blade sank deep into his flesh; his hands went numb, and he was no longer able to hold the gun; it fell to the floor with a loud clattering noise that echoed throughout the room. Salvatore collapsed, blood seeping through his clothes.

The nurse stood over him, her eyes gleaming, 'Nobody can defeat me,' she taunted.

Ramello watched with a mix of shock and terror; he felt paralysed. The nurse reached for her phone, dialling a number with practised ease. 'Hi, RD,' she purred.

'What's up, girl?' RD asked.

'Salvatore's in the hospital, and I've stabbed the fool,' the nurse laughed, 'And the boy's here as well.'

'How'd they end up there, fam?' RD asked.

'Figure it out yourself,' the nurse snapped, 'Are you going to come or not?'

'Aight, I'm on my way,' RD said lazily, putting the phone down.

Taking advantage of the distraction, Salvatore grabbed his gun from the floor and fired; the shot rang, and the nurse fell, clutching her arm and screaming in agony.

Salvatore grabbed Ramello's hand, 'We need to get out of here,' he stammered, the pain from the wound in his pain searing up his body.

They ran out of the room and down a corridor. 'You're limping badly, boy. Are you alright?' Salvatore observed.

'Not too good,' Ramello replied with a painful moan.

They ran out of the hospital and into the car park where Salvatore's SUV was parked.

'What happened to VD?' Ramello asked as they sat in the car.

'Please don't talk about that loser; he's no concern to you,' Salvatore replied, turning the car on.

'You better tell me before I do something nasty to you,' Ramello shouted.

'You're a very rude boy, lad,' Salvatore said, 'Anyway, he got one hundred and one bullets in his body, and he is going to be in the hospital for a long time,' he said, ending his sentence with a laugh.

Ramello stayed quiet and stared out of the window.

'Can I ask you something, boy?' Salvatore asked, 'How come you act like VD is your dad? What has he done for you?'

Ramello tried to think but could only remember VD wiping his tears away and helping him up from Me's attack. 'I don't really know, I just like him,' he replied.

Salvatore sighed and rolled his eyes, 'You're a very strange lad.'

Salvatore drove on until they arrived at his house, 'You can sleep in my house for the night,' he said with an exhausted sigh.

They jumped out of the car and walked towards the front door. Ramello looked at the mansion's façade; it was safeguarded by smart security cameras, motion sensors, and alarms. Ramello was shocked when Salvatore opened the door without a key. The door had a smart lock, and he opened it with a personalised code. Salvatore led him into the dining room.

'You stay in my dining room,' Salvatore instructed, 'My side is killing me from that damn stab wound,' he confessed, pressing a hand against his blood-soaked shirt. 'It's still bleeding. I need to tend to it.'

Ramello nodded and watched as Salvatore left the room. He looked around the dining room, which was connected to the kitchen by double sliding glass doors. Through the glass doors, glimpses of the kitchen revealed a marble countertop, gleaming stainless-steel appliances, and a row of fragrant herbs on the windowsill. His gaze fell on the table, its surface adorned with a vase of fresh flowers. He liked Salvatore's house a lot.

He realised that Salvatore's home illuminated intelligently. The lights adjusted based on time of day, occupancy, or voice commands.

After a bit, Salvatore returned. His dark hair was damp, clinging to his forehead from the shower he had taken. He looked at Ramello. 'I'll get you some supper,' he said, disappearing into the kitchen.

Ramello leaned back in his chair, content in the quiet companionship of this unfamiliar yet strangely comforting house. It was more than a place to stay; it was a haven, a refuge from the chaos beyond the walls.

Salvatore walked back into the room with two bowls of pasta in his hands. He put them on the table, 'Eat, boy,' he commanded, sitting on a chair opposite Ramello.

Ramello started to eat and then asked, 'Do you live alone in this house?'

Salvatore nodded, 'Yes, I live alone; why do you ask?'

'Because the house is massive,' Ramello replied, 'Listen, I want to tell you something.'

'What is it?' Salvatore asked.

'My brothers have been forced to join VD,' Ramello confessed.

Salvatore's silence was heavy, 'How do you know?'

Ramello sighed, 'Because I rang my brother, Edmond, and VD picked it up,' he explained.

They spoke briefly, and then Salvatore said, 'Get some rest; it's getting late.'

Ramello yawned lazily, 'Yeah, I've had a long day today.'

Salvatore led him to his room, and as soon as his head hit the pillow, he fell asleep.

Ramello suddenly woke up; he could hear Salvatore's voice booming from outside. He rubbed his eyes, walked to the window, and peered out.

He could see Salvatore standing in the street. Police cars were parked near the house, their flashing lights painting the night sky.

'I'm coming back,' Salvatore shouted at one of the officers, then walked back into his house.

Ramello settled back in the bed, wondering what had triggered this strange commotion. The bedroom door swung open, and Salvatore stormed in. Ramello turned to him, 'What's all the racket about?' he asked.

'The racket?' Salvatore bellowed, 'I'm going to have to go down to the station; I'm being taken in for questioning.'

'What have you done?' Ramello asked curiously.

Salvatore stared directly at him, 'You look pleased,' he sneered, 'Anyway, it's just for the night because of that rubbish that happened in the hospital, and tomorrow, I have to go to court. Take this, lad,' he said, passing Ramello a piece of paper, 'Hold onto this code; it's for the smart lock in case you need to unlock the door.'

'So, what am I meant to do on my own?' Ramello asked.

'You stay in the house and get whatever you want from the kitchen,' Salvatore instructed, then stormed back out of the room.

Ramello grabbed his phone from the nightstand and went into his WhatsApp. He was itching to phone one of his brothers, so he rang Frederik, wondering who would pick it up.

The phone connected, but silence hung on the line.

'Frederick,' Ramello whispered, 'Is it you or that evil devil again?'

There was a noisy smirk from the other side, but the person didn't answer.

'Frederick,' Ramello shouted, 'I know it's you.'

'Yeah, it is me,' Frederick finally replied, 'What do you want?'

'Where are you?' Ramello insisted.

'None of your business,' Frederick shot back, 'I was wondering where you have disappeared to.'

'Is VD there?' Ramello's voice trembled.

'No, he isn't here. I've been told he's in the hospital, and anyway, why do you want to know about his whereabouts?' Frederick replied.

'Oh yeah! How can I forget he got shot in the leg? That's why he must have admitted himself into the hospital,' Ramello said grimly.

'Why are you phoning me at this time?' Frederick asked, 'You know I shouldn't be talking to you.'

'Frederick,' Ramello sighed, 'How come you joined VD? Overall, he is a bad guy.'

After a long silence, Frederick snapped, 'Don't ever ask me questions like these ever again, Ramello.'

'Why?' Ramello shouted, 'What have you got to hide from me?'

'VD told me not to speak to you, and he's going to shoot me dead if he finds out I'm speaking to you, and I will break your face if he finds out,' Frederick shouted back.

'Yeah, you can break my face if you're still alive,' Ramello replied, disconnecting the call.

Ramello sat in disappointment and felt betrayed by those he was close to.

Chapter 9
Park Standoff

The morning light filtered through the curtains, casting a pale glow on Ramello's face. He slowly got up out of the bed and walked down the marble stairs.

He finishing his breakfast, which was like a king's dinner. Salvatore had everything you could imagine in his kitchen. He entered the living room and sat on a lovely, comfortable chair.

He looked out the window and watched the world outside, the passing cars and the sound of the noisy streets. He wondered what would happen to Salvatore; imagine he was sentenced to a few years; then, where would he go?

Suddenly, his phone rang. He realised it was Salvatore's number, which Salvatore had given him the day before.

'Hello,' answered Ramello.

'Where are you?' Salvatore asked.

'In your house, sitting in the living room all bored,' Ramello replied.

'Good,' Salvatore said, 'Make sure you stay there. I will send you someone's number, so if you need something, give him a bell, OK?'

'OK,' Ramello replied, 'Where are you now?'

'I'm heading into court in an hour,' Salvatore replied.

'I hope you don't get a long sentence,' Ramello said.

'I'll make sure I don't go down,' Salvatore laughed, 'You don't worry about me, and anyway, it wasn't my fault; it was that witch who pulled out the knife first.'

'Yeah,' Ramello sighed, 'But you know people aren't getting proper justice nowadays. Do you know who the judge is going to be?' Ramello asked.

'It's going to be my mate, and he is known for making good decisions,' Salvatore said.

'So, you've got a good chance then,' Ramello replied.

'Anyway, boy, I need to go,' Salvatore said, 'Bye.'

Ramello moved the phone away from his ear and looked around his surroundings, sighing.

Suddenly his phone rang again, he looked at it and realised it was Salvatore again.

He picked it up, 'Hi.'

'Sorry for bothering you again; I just wanted to tell you that if you need something, there's a shop at the bottom of the street; you can always go there to shop, but you have to get back home straight away without hanging around, got it?' Salvatore said.

'No problem, I'll do that,' Ramello replied, turning the phone off.

He thought for a while, then decided to pop into the corner shop to pass some time. He walked towards the front door, where he found his trainers.

He opened the door, locked it, and walked down the baking-hot street.

Upon entering the shop, he wandered around for a while and walked out without buying anything.

He preceded back up the street, past Salvatore's house, thinking to himself, what a lovely walk.

He entered a nearby park and leaned against a tree, looking at the sky. 'The weather is beautiful,' he said, the soft breeze brushing against his skin.

'Yeah, it's definitely very beautiful, isn't it?' a voice said behind him.

Ramello spun around, startled, and standing behind him was Me and another guy. Me's dark, midnight eyes seemed to pierce him, his raven-black hair falling in waves across his forehead.

'What are you doing here?' Me taunted.

Ramello looked at him, dread filling his heart.

'Lost your voice box, eh?' Me jeered, 'I think we should service it.'

The other man laughed, 'Cat got your tongue, boy. I'm going to fix it.' He approached Ramello and grabbed him by the collar, 'What are you doing here? Tell me before I end you.'

'Leave him to me, Austin,' Me interrupted, he shoved Austin out of the way, and looked into Ramello's eyes, 'How did that bullet feel which I shot into your leg at the police station?' he grinned evilly.

'It felt great,' Ramello shouted, 'Now leave me alone; I've given you the answer.'

Me looked at Austin, and then they both shared a laugh, 'Ha! You really think I'm going to let you off the hook,' Me taunted, 'Let me show you what I'm going to do with you.' He yanked Ramello closer and threw a punch in his face; blood sprayed out from Ramello's nose.

But this time Ramello wasn't going to let Me go either, filled with anger; his fist met Me's face with vengeance; he grabbed Me's face and dug his nails into the flesh around the eyes, refusing to let go. Me's scream vibrated around the park, but Ramello didn't care. He withdrew his hands, leaving a trail of nail marks printed on his face.

'How did that feel?' Ramello yelled and grabbed Me's hair, pulling it till Me's eyes started to shed tears.

'Help me, Austin!' Me screeched with agony, but Ramello didn't give up.

Austin charged from behind and attempted to separate them, but Ramello's grip on Me was firm.

'Get his filthy claws off my hair,' Me shouted.

Austin, always the joker, chuckled, 'I'm trying, bro,' he said, 'You gonna be bold, and you're going to look ugly after this.'

'I don't care how ugly I look; just get him off!' Me screamed.

Finally, after a frantic struggle, Austin managed to move Ramello, who was panting like crazy.

Me's face had turned bright red, and he looked vexed.

'How did that feel?' Ramello asked him with a smirk.

'It felt like a lovely massage,' Me shouted.

'Then why were you screaming and yelling and begging for help like a bitch?' Ramello replied.

'Don't be a smartass,' Me said through clenched teeth, drawing a gun from his IWB holster, 'You're going to regret that you even spoke to me.'

'Shoot me, you scrag!' Ramello shouted, 'I've got nothing to lose.'

'You might not have anything to lose, but other people have a lot to lose,' he said, hinting at something which confused Ramello even more. Me sniggered. His eyes bore into Ramello's, a silent threat.

Both Ramello and Me were staring into each other's eyes when Austin's sudden scream shattered the standoff.

Me looked at him, 'What are you screaming at, you weirdo?' he asked.

Austin didn't reply; he stood motionless, gripping his gun and looking at someone approaching them.

Me squinted, narrowing his eyes at the figure. Suddenly, his heart started to pound fast, 'Come on, Austin, we need to get out of here,' he bellowed; Austin shot a bullet at the person, but it bounced off the man's chest like a ping-pong ball.

'You stupid twit!' Me's frustration erupted, 'He's wearing a bulletproof jacket.'

'Why don't I just shoot him in the legs or the head, then?' Austin retorted swiftly.

'Shut up, we need to get out of here,' Me yelled.

Austin and Me legged it without looking back, leaving Ramello behind in the park.

Ramello's gaze shifted towards the approaching person, hoping he wasn't harbouring ill intentions.

The man drew closer; he was of middle height, with dark brown hair, and was dressed in black except for his bright white Nike Airs adorned with red ticks.

The man didn't look menacing, but Ramello's anxiety started to increase. Should he run or stay put?

The man stopped in front of Ramello and sighed, 'Greetings, boy,' he said.

Ramello felt paralysed under the man's gaze, 'Hi,' he replied, his voice barely escaping his throat.

'You're such a disobedient boy,' the man again sighed, his voice a low rumble, 'Why didn't you just stay put in Salvatore's house when he told you clearly not to leave?'

Ramello gulped. He didn't know how to address this strange man. How did he know that Salvatore told him to stay inside his house? 'Who are you?' he asked.

The man smiled, hesitated, then said, 'The phone number Salvatore provided you belongs to me.'

Ramello nodded in acknowledgement.

'So, tell me why you left the house,' the man enquired again.

'I...I just wanted to stretch my legs,' Ramello stammered, a shiver in his voice, 'Please don't tell Salvatore.'

'I don't keep secrets,' the man laughed. 'Rules exist for a reason, my boy. Now, let's get you back home.'

Ramello and the man started to walk towards Salvatore's house. Ramello glanced at him several times and realised his uncanny resemblance with Salvatore.

'You and Salvatore look very alike,' Ramello blurted out, unable to contain his curiosity; he stared at the man, who suddenly started feeling uncomfortable.

'Dya really think so?' the man smiled nervously. They arrived at the house and entered the living room, where they seated themselves on a luxurious sofa.

'What's your name?' Ramello asked.

'You can call me Lenny,' the man replied with a strange grin.

'Lenny,' Ramello repeated, his curiosity piqued, 'What kind of name is that?'

Lenny leaned back, his fingers tracing the patterns on the sofa, 'It's not my actual name,' he confessed, 'People just call me Lenny.'

After speaking for a while, Lenny looked towards the window, 'I need to go now,' he murmured, rising from the sofa, 'but make sure you stay in the house; Salvatore already told me how much of a pest you are.'

Ramello nodded, feeling a sudden sense of isolation as he watched Lenny walk out of the room and leave the house. The door clicked shut, sealing them both in their separate worlds.

He then lay flat on the sofa and stared at the ceiling. He had nothing to do, and he knew that Lenny would be keeping an eye on the house.

Ramello slowly closed his eyes, thinking about Lenny, who had vanished in the brightness of the day, leaving behind questions and echoes of a name that held many secrets than meets the eye. Then, Ramello fell fast asleep.

Chapter 10
The Old Repeat

'Ramello! Ramello! Get up!'

Ramello's eyes snapped open; he could hear someone calling his name. He looked at the person who was standing near the window and realised it was Lenny.

'How did you get in the house?' Ramello asked, his voice edged with caution.

'Well, I knocked on the door,' Lenny explained, leaning against a wall, 'But then I realised that the door was unlocked, and that's how I got in, and I'm distraught that you hadn't locked it after I left, you clumsy person.'

'Sorry, I didn't realise, I thought it locks auto,' Ramello apologised. 'But why have you come back?'

'Because Salvatore told me that he's been consistently ringing you and wants to know why you ain't picking up,' Lenny replied in an annoyed tone.

'And why's he been ringing me?' asked Ramello.

Lenny came closer, and Ramello could feel his breath against his cheek, 'He wanted to tell you that he should be returning tonight, and he wanted to check up on you,' he answered, 'And also, he is very pissed you left the house.'

'Why did you tell him?' Ramello asked, annoyed.

'Because I had to tell him you left the house without permission when you shouldn't have,' Lenny grinned.

'You didn't have to tell him?' Ramello shouted, his voice trembling.

'Don't raise your voice at me, Boy,' Lenny warned. 'I'm no ordinary guy you're going to boss about; I'm a guy who will sort your attitude out. So, you better straighten out that stinking attitude of yours.'

'Why did you tell him?' Ramello repeated, trying to control his temper.

'I already told you that I'm going to tell him; I wasn't joking,' Lenny retorted, his voice as sharp as broken glass.

Ramello sighed, 'Fine, I'll just get beaten up into a pulp when he returns, and you better make sure you're there to watch the show,' he snapped.

Lenny laughed, 'I won't be around for that; I've got a busy schedule, and anyway, you should be happy I was there to save your ass when I did,' he said.

'I could have saved myself,' Ramello shot back, giving him withered looks.

'Mind your manners, you rude piece of work,' Lenny said, raising his voice, 'If you speak to me with this kind of shitty attitude again, I'm going to beat the crap out of you, well and proper.'

'Do what you want with me,' Ramello shouted arrogantly, his voice harsh, 'I don't have a life anyway, I live like a scrag who clearly doesn't know how to look after himself.'

Lenny glared at him attentively, then turned around and walked out of the room, 'Make sure you don't forget to lock the door this time,' he yelled, his words echoing in the empty hallway as he walked out of the house.

Ramello stomped towards the door and locked it with the code Salvatore had given him. He then barged up the stairs and into his bedroom, angry and annoyed, flinging himself on the bed.

'Only if I had got shot dead!' he shouted into the empty room, 'I would have been better off than living with these horrible people.'

He screamed to himself for ages till he started dozing off. He tried to shake the tiredness away and sat up, resting his head on his knees, but sleep still overcame him.

After a long time, he jolted awake and realised night had fallen; he swiftly jumped out of bed and dashed down the stairs. He entered the living room and found his phone ringing on the coffee table, 'Hello,' he answered breathlessly.

'You dumb boy,' Salvatore thundered, his wrath erupting like a volcano, 'You never seem to pick the phone up. What's wrong with you?'

'Sorry, I fell asleep,' Ramello replied, yawning loudly.

'Lazy fool,' Salvatore sighed, 'When I phoned you earlier, you ignored me; Lenny told me that you were sleeping then as well, and now you're sleeping again! Are you not well?'

'No, I'm not feeling good,' Ramello shouted, 'I'm feeling depressed here.'

Salvatore's voice hardened. 'Listen, boy,' he barked. 'I'm on my way home. Brace yourself; I'm going to unleash my fury when I arrive. Lenny spilled your secrets.'

Ramello didn't answer and slammed the phone down; he sat on a sofa and sighed; he didn't understand who on earth these men were and what they wanted from him. On top of that, Salvatore and Lenny were two sides of the same coin, both bearing the same personalities he hated.

Suddenly, the front door unlocked, and Salvatore entered the living room. 'Hi, boy,' he said, his eyes betraying warmth; they bore into Ramello like twin daggers.

'Hello,' Ramello replied, his voice dripping with attitude.

Salvatore sat in a chair opposite Ramello and looked him directly in the eyes. Ramello stared back, not caring what he had to say.

'Lad,' Salvatore said, 'Look down before I gouge those eyes out for you.'

Ramello held his gaze but didn't reply.

'I said look down before I poke your dirty eyes out,' Salvatore roared.

'I'm not going to listen to you,' Ramello shouted back. 'I'm sick of all this!'

'That's it, boy, I'm sick of you giving me this shit!' Salvatore yelled, standing up and crossing the room in swift strides. Like iron talons, his fingers clamped onto Ramello's collar, lifting him off the sofa. 'If you don't want to listen to what I've got to say,' he spat out, 'then get the hell out of my house. I've done so much for you, and you have the nerve to treat me like this?'

Ramello looked at him, 'Fine,' he retorted, 'I'm going, and yeah, you expect me to stay in your house when I don't even truly know who you are, I'm going, and I know I'll be better off.'

Salvatore dragged him to the front door, forced his trainers on, and opened the door, revealing the night beyond. Salvatore pushed him into the darkness and slammed the door in his face—the same way RD had slammed the door on his face before, the noise echoing like a gunshot.

The garden blurred as he sprinted down the road; at least I can walk freely, he thought bitterly.

He ran through many streets, wondering where he would end up. He finally ended up in an alley where he sat down for a rest; he was tired from all the pains and aches. He wrapped his arms around his legs, and rested his head on his knees. Tears dripped onto his knees, and he started to feel guilty. Suddenly, a man walked into the alley, his eyes lingering on Ramello, but he didn't say anything and continued walking; Ramello did not like how he stared at him. He wiped his tears away with his sleeve and stood up; he knew he had to find somewhere to sleep for the night. He got to the end of the alley and looked around; he needed to find out where Salvatore's house was but couldn't recognise the area. He walked into a narrow, filthy street that looked like a trash yard and continued walking until he turned into another street, but as he looked around, he saw a suspicious figure striding towards him. Suddenly, someone came from behind and yanked him backwards. Ramello screamed with fright; he didn't know who these men were, and it was pretty difficult to see through the darkness.

Suddenly, he heard the man behind him loudly growl, 'Leave the boy alone.'

The man in front of Ramello gave a horse-like laugh, 'You get your hands off the boy,' he said, his voice close to a whisper. He walked up to Ramello and yanked him away from the man who was holding him from behind. Ramello looked up at the man and saw his eyes glowing red; he gulped, more scared than ever; it was RD.

'Move away from the boy,' the man who was behind commanded.

'Violence suits me,' RD scoffed, pulling Ramello further away, 'You claim to be a hardcore? Well, step up and get him; he's your prize.'

'You know I live up to my name,' the other man declared, his voice echoing like a distant storm, 'Give him to me.'

Ramello's scared eyes looked up at the other man and realised it was, in fact, VD.

RD tightened his grip around Ramello's throat, putting his gun to his head, 'You try to even move one millimetre more forward, and I'm gonna shoot him dead, then you can have his dead body because I'm not gonna need him anymore,' he laughed, Ramello started gasping for air as RD continued to apply pressure to his neck.

VD looked at him in the eyes and said:

> 'Back off, leave the kid alone,
> This ain't your playground; it's ma throne.
> Ya think you're tough, ya think you're bold?
> I'm the legend here; ma story's told.
> So, take this rhyme as your final warning,
> Disappear by night, gone by morning.
> So, let me make it clear and right.
> Hit the gas, vanish into the night.'

RD stared at VD, his eyes glowing with hatred, 'I ain't no kid, so stop tryna sing me songs, and get to the point; if you come close, I'm going to shoot him dead,' he spat.

'Listen, RD,' VD said, his voice calm, 'The boy's innocent, so let him go, and we'll have a one-to-one.'

'What are you chattin' about?' RD scoffed, 'Lemme tell ya, this thick idiot ain't a bystander; he's part of this game.'

In a matter of seconds, Ramello noticed someone coming from behind VD. He was going to scream, but RD quickly covered his mouth with his hand and whispered, 'You need to keep your fat yap shut; it's so big that you can trap a well-fed rat in there.'

Suddenly, VD screamed, his body stiff with pain as he fell to the ground, grabbing his back. RD's laughter echoed, cruel and triumphant. Ramello realised Me was standing behind VD with a knife in his hands.

'How'd that feel?' RD laughed and kicked VD in the face, who was writhing on the ground, screaming with a mixture of irritation and agony.

'Ain't no one gonna put me on my back foot,' RD declared, his vampire canines showing. 'Now you can stay there and die a horrible death whilst I take the boy with me,' he turned towards Me, 'You did a good job, Ace.'

Me looked at Ramello with his cunning eyes as Ramello acknowledged his actual name.

VD's eyes met Ramello's, 'Try to escape from RD when you get the chance,' he mouthed silently, loud enough for Ramello to hear.

'What are we going to do with the boy?' Ace asked.

'Imma toss him in ma whip, straight up,' RD laughed; he grabbed Ramello's arm and started to stroll down the street, followed by Ace.

They walked to the end of the street, where the same red SUV was parked. RD took his keys out of his pocket and opened the car. 'Hop in, little homie. This is ma whip,' he beckoned, holding open the back door for Ramello.

'I'm never going to come with you!' Ramello shouted, taking a step backwards away from RD, but Ace grabbed his arm, flinging him into the back seats and slammed the door shut.

Ramello knew he had no choice. He watched as RD and Ace hopped into the front. RD started the car.

'Where are you going to take me now?' Ramello asked, fear hitting his heart like sharp daggers.

RD gave an exaggerated eye roll, 'Same lame question,' he sighed, steering the car onto the road. 'You're full of shit, boy.'

'How come you lot always catch up to me?' Ramello shouted in frustration.

RD cracked up, 'Spies,' he spat. 'We watchin' your every move, no matter where you're at. And that VD? Man, he's creepin' in the shadows, always super-glued to me, like a pesky mosquito. Straight-up annoying as hell.'

Ramello slumped into his seat and pulled his legs up.

'Take your pongy trainers off my bleedin' car's seats!' RD remarked angrily.

Ramello glanced up; RD's gaze bore into him through the main mirror. He quickly obeyed, knowing RD's obsession with his polished cars could lead him to even more trouble.

They drove on for a long time. At this point, Ramello felt very depressed and decided the best thing to do was to meet his fate with open arms; it wasn't looking good for him; it felt like a repeat of what had happened to him before, and he realised they were driving on the same motorway. 'Blimey!' he thought, 'Same repeat!'

'This journey is taking ages,' Ramello complained, stretching lazily.

'Keep dreamin', kid,' RD sneered, 'Cuz when we hit our spot, you'll be six feet under.'

Ramello stayed quiet; he didn't like the sound of the threat. He would probably get killed, and there was no Salvatore to save him this time.

Many hours passed when suddenly, RD swerved and drove the car into a huge driveway. Ramello looked out of the window and realised they were back at RD's house. RD and Ace leapt out; RD opened Ramello's door, who slowly, like a slug, got out of the car.

'You need to stop wasting time, boy,' RD snapped, delivering a blow to Ramello's head, 'You're toddlin' around like a bleedin' tot!'

Ramello followed the two men into the grand house.

'Kick them grimy kicks off, or I'll do it for ya!' RD barked.

Ramello quickly took his trainers off and followed them into the living room. He looked around and saw RD's son, Ander, sitting on one of the sofas doing something on his phone, behaving like his dad had never shot him; they seemed happy together.

Ander looked up at Ramello but just smiled and looked back down.

'What's the craic, Ander?' RD inquired; he walked over to a mirror and combed his fringe back with his hand, ensuring a single strand wasn't out of place.

'Nothing important, Dad,' Ander replied, putting his phone into his pocket, and gazing at his stylish dad, who was fussing around with his hair.

'Yo, paralysed kid, park it. You aren't impressin' anybody just standin' there. I can't see anyone's jaws droppin' watchin' ya,' RD said sharply, looking at Ramello from the side of his eyes.

Ramello slowly sat down on one of the plush sofas and sank into its comfort.

RD turned around and started walking up and down the length of the room, thinking thoughtfully. He finally looked at Ramello, whose eyes were watching every step he took, 'What are ya starin' at, lad?' he asked.

'I'm staring at you, who else?' Ramello replied.

RD laughed, the sound echoing from the lavish walls, 'Yo, mark ma words, you know that cheekiness of yours? It's 'bout to burst out like a soda can!'

Ramello glared at him, 'Yeah, whatever, how are you going to take my cheekiness out of me?' he challenged.

RD sighed and sat down near him, 'Listen up, kiddo,' he said, for once, his face didn't look so evil, 'Ever wonder why the whole bleedin' planet's hot on your tail?' his voice dropped lower, 'It's like you're the last doughnut and everyone wants a piece. So, spill the beans, Sunshine. What's your secret sauce? Why's the world playin' hide and seek with ya?'

Ramello shook his head, 'I don't know.'

RD nodded and leaned closer to him, 'Now lemme tell ya, it ain't about you, it's all about your pops.'

'But I don't have a dad,' Ramello protested, 'So what has he got to do with me?'

RD smiled, 'Yo, you've got a pops, but nobody's got a clue where the jerk is at. So, the only shot is to snatch you up and make you spill the beans, 'cause you're his son, and after all, you probably have information that you ain't sharin', ya feel me?'

'Yes, I understand you very well, but I don't know where he is,' Ramello replied, then gestured to his phone, 'Check if you want, I've got nobody's number saved as 'Dad.'

Suddenly Ramello's phone started to ring, he looked at it and realised it was Salvatore.

'Who's that?' asked RD.

'Salvatore,' Ramello replied.

'Pick it up, turn on the speaker mode and peep what he's gotta tell ya,' RD said, leaning back and putting his arms behind his head, waiting for Ramello to answer.

Ramello sighed and answered the phone, turning on the speaker mode. 'Hi, Salvatore, what do you want?' he asked.

'Where are you, lad?' Salvatore asked worriedly, 'I've searched the streets for you, but you're nowhere to be seen.'

'Why are you trying to find me?' Ramello retorted, 'Have you not had enough with me?'

'No, no,' Salvatore said calmly, 'Look, kid, I'm deeply sorry for kicking you out of the house; it was just the heat of the moment.'

'Well, your apologies won't change anything now, I'm already trapped in RD's house,' Ramello replied abruptly.

Silence hung on the other end for a moment, then Salvatore erupted, 'What did you say?' he screamed, 'I hope you're not playing thick games with me.'

RD's laughter filled the room as he snatched the phone from Ramello's hand, 'Hi, Salvatore,' he greeted.

'You son of a bitch! You better let the boy go!' Salvatore shouted, which made RD snigger.

'I ain't releasin' him,' RD growled. 'If he ain't spillin' the beans about his old man, then I'm comin' for you 'cause I know ya got the answers.'

'Fine,' Salvatore said, trying to keep his tone cool. 'Let the boy go, and then we will talk face-to-face; I will not be calling again, and I'm giving you a last chance.'

'Nah, fam, it ain't rollin' like that,' RD declared, 'I'm holdin' onto the kid, ya feel me? We gonna link up, and I'm gonna bring the boy with me, then we'll talk; our convo ain't gonna be mere words; it's gonna be about life and death.'

'No, you're going to let the boy go first,' Salvatore persisted.

Ramello listened to the two debating for ages and was starting to get a headache. Quickly, he snatched the phone from RD's grasp and said, 'Listen, there's no need to fight because he is not going to let me go free.'

'I've had enough of this nonsense,' Salvatore shouted, slamming the phone down.

Ramello looked at RD, 'Now, what are you planning to do with me?' he demanded.

RD stared at him, 'What ya on about?'

'You brought me here. Now tell me what your intention is,' Ramello snapped.

'I gotcha a spot for the night, then we'll speak tomorrow,' RD replied.

'I'm calling a night as well,' Ace declared, standing up and shaking RD's hands. He then walked out of the room and left.

'You lads better behave yourselves; I gotta hit the bathroom,' RD bellowed.

Ramello started observing Ander, who was fidgeting with his phone. Ander looked up at him curiously, 'Why are you looking at me with so much studiousness?' he asked.

'It's nothing,' Ramello smiled, ashamed that he had been noticed, 'But I did want to ask how old you are.'

Ander sighed, 'I'm turning eighteen next month, and I'm dreading it,' he confessed.

'Why are you dreading it?' Ramello asked, confused.

'Just,' Ander's voice dropped, and then fearfully, he glanced at the door, 'Dad said I have to do jobs for him, you know, I gotta step up and live up to the family name,' he explained.

'What kind of jobs?' Ramello asked.

'He wants me to continue his legacy by being a gangster,' Ander replied, shrugging his shoulders, 'Anyway, no more talking before I get into trouble.'

Ramello nodded and looked at Ander, still playing with his jocker-blocker phone.

After a while, RD reappeared, 'I think it's time for ya to bounce to yer crib,' he said, looking at Ramello, who was dozing off on the sofa.

Ramello stood up and followed RD into a massive and inviting room that was not on the top floor.

Without hesitation, Ramello sprinted towards a double-sized bed, collapsed on it, and fell asleep. With a huge sigh, RD stared at him, then turned around and left the room, locking the door from the outside.

Chapter 11
A Bloodied Fight

The following morning, Ramello was called for breakfast. He walked out of the bedroom and tried to navigate the way to the kitchen; the house was huge.

He finally came across glass doors, which he entered, and with shock and awe, he realised he was standing in the kitchen. He glanced towards the table and saw RD, Ander and a girl sitting around it. They all looked at him like curious scientists, making him nervous.

'Sit down, young blood,' RD's voice sliced through the air, his amber eyes piercing into Ramello's.

Ramello sat down near him and stared at the food; it didn't look very appealing.

He sat there staring at it for ages, then RD probed, 'Yo, why ya ain't eating?'

'Because I don't feel like it,' Ramello replied.

RD sighed and stood up, 'I'm comin' back; gotta get myself sorted,' he said, then turned to the girl, 'Tidy up the kitchen, Dalayza, and Ander, lend her a hand.'

They both nodded and watched as their dad walked out of the room.

Dalayza stood up and started to wash the dishes, and Ander helped clear the table while Ramello watched the show.

After a while, they finished cleaning and started talking to each other in low voices, making it impossible for Ramello to hear.

Suddenly, the kitchen doors swung open, and there stood RD. He was dressed in black, and his red contact lenses were glowing.

'Y'all finished?' he asked.

Dalayza and Ander nodded.

'A'ight,' RD's voice cut through the room, 'Let's slide to the livin' room; I got some words for Ramello.'

Ramello started to feel nervous; he dreaded what RD had to say to him. They walked out of the kitchen and into the living room.

He sat on the sofa on which he had rested the day before, and RD sat opposite him, with Dalayza and Ander seated on either side, which made him even more nervous.

RD brushed his silky hair away from his face and then said in a rough, horrible voice, 'Don't worry, young blood, ain't gonna coddle ya like I did last night, but now it's time for ya to get your face broken, which mirrors your old man's.'

Ramello heard Dalayza give out a witchy laugh, making him angry, but he remained silent.

RD stood up and circled the sofa on which Ramello was sitting, 'Yo, lad, I wonder where your rotten dad is?' he asked, blowing his ciggy breath into Ramello's face.

Ramello angrily grabbed his head, 'I don't know,' he said.

'A'ight, since you ain't got a clue, I'ma blast you straight outta here and drop you in hell,' RD replied seriously.

The threat hung in the air; Ramello felt scared and suffocated, 'Do what you want with me,' he replied, his voice trembling.

RD looked at Ander, who stood up and walked over to Ramello. RD sat back down, observing the unfolding scene as if it were a gripping movie. Ander grabbed Ramello by the arm and flung him to the floor; his head hit the living room table, making his vision hazy. As blood trickled down his forehead, Ramello quickly stood up and ran in the opposite direction, but RD stuck his leg out, and Ramello went flying onto the floor. He tried to get up, but Ander slammed him down with one punch, and then he heard Dalayza repeat the same witchy laugh, mocking his helplessness. He grabbed his nose, which was severely bleeding, staining the carpet crimson. Each blow felt like a betrayal, a reminder of his vulnerability. His mouth filled with the metallic taste of blood, causing him to choke up blood, 'Stop!' he gasped, the words escaping between ragged breaths as blood trickled down his chin, 'Get away from me!'

'Why shall I get away from you? You loser!' Ander mockingly laughed, 'I'm going to make sure you don't see daylight again.'

A final punch to the chest stole Ramello's breath away.

Amused by his son's performance, RD signalled for Ander to stop; they laughed at Ramello's battered face.

Ander walked away. RD grabbed Ramello's arm and made him sit on the sofa, 'How'd it feel boy?' he laughed, looking at Ramello's flabbergasted expression.

Ramello's tears streamed down his face, blurring his vision. He felt utterly helpless, like a vulnerable infant crying for his mother's comforting embrace, 'Just leave me alone,' he sobbed, locking eyes with RD, 'I've done nothing wrong to you, that I deserve this.'

RD's amusement twisted into something darker; he pulled a gun from his jeans pocket, the cold metal pressing against Ramello's temple, 'You're gonna regret that you even exist,' he hissed, slamming the weapon into Ramello's head. Pain exploded in Ramello's head, and he yelled out of agony. RD looked into his eyes, 'I'm gonna make sure you die a dirty death, and you go six feet under, but I'm gonna make sure I still get my hands on your cursed dad; he's one jerk just like you,' he sneered, then with sudden force, he smashed Ramello's head into the table.

Ramello's thoughts swirled in a haze; his skull felt like mashed potatoes, and he wondered if he'd ever see straight again. Suddenly, Ramello's phone rang, and RD extracted it from his pocket.

'Yo,' he heard RD's voice, 'Can I help you, BFG?'

'BFG?' Salvatore's voice erupted from the other end. 'Who the hell is BFG? And where's Ramello?'

'Your boy, Ramello, can't come to the phone right now 'cause he's all messed up in ma crib,' RD laughed, 'And I'm gonna send him to the afterlife.'

'Don't even think about putting your crooked fingers on him,' Salvatore shouted, 'I'll rearrange your face.'

'Try it; ain't nobody knows where I live,' RD taunted.

'Do you remember when you said that, and I caught up to you at 200 South Orange?' Salvatore shouted, 'I'm going to find you.'

'Look, Bruh, if you ever track me down, you're gonna see Ramello dead in front of your snobby eyes,' RD laughed, 'Wanna hear the punk scream?' he asked, slamming the butt of the gun into Ramello's face again, his nose and lip started bleeding as he screamed with pain at the top of his lungs.

'Did ya hear him?' RD laughed, 'He ain't got long to live.'

Salvatore slammed the phone down, unwilling to hear anything further.

RD looked at the phone and then, with anger, threw it across the room, making it shatter on the wall, 'Now let's see who's got the bloody guts to call,' he muttered, throwing a punch at Ramello's face.

Ramello sat up, his head spinning, and grabbed RD's blood-slicked hand, 'Please, can you stop?' he pleaded.

'Why should I quit?' RD laughed and was just about to punch him again when he remembered something. He stopped himself, made the sobbing Ramello sit back on the sofa, and started staring at him without even blinking until Ander had to interrupt, 'What's up, Dad?'

RD gave his son daggers, and it seemed like he might throw a punch in Ander's face, 'Zip it,' he snapped, 'Before I crack that mug of yours.'

Ander's sigh of arrogance hung in the air, and his gaze shifted back to Ramello. 'So, what are you going to do with the busted lad?' he asked his dad.

RD didn't answer but stood up and walked over to Ramello's shattered phone. Its shattered form was a testament to the violence that had just happened. He picked it up, took the back part off, pulled the SIM and memory card out, and inserted them into his phone while Ramello's phone found its final resting place in the bin. He started to fiddle with his phone; his facial expressions beat every kind of expression in the book.

'What are you looking at, Dad?' Ander asked suspiciously.

'Nothin', Ander, can you just zip your big gob up,' RD barked.

Ander's annoyance flared. RD was a master of evasion, withholding answers like precious secrets.

RD walked up to Ramello who was still sobbing, and sat near him, 'Listen, boy,' he said, 'What's all this rubbish?'

Ramello looked at his phone. RD was reading his notes, and some of his writings were about weird stuff. But the section RD was looking at made his stomach turn, 'Stop being nosey in my business,' Ramello replied.

RD's eyes narrowed. 'Your whole life is full of disaster,' he mused, scanning the names on the screen. 'And who's this Jeffery cat?'

'I don't know,' Ramello's shout echoed. 'Stop going through my stuff.'

'Yo, you're definitely tellin' me who this Jeffery guy is 'cause you hollered at me,' RD snapped, 'And I'm gonna dig through everythin' of yours.'

'To be honest, Jeffery is someone I've heard of, but I do not know him,' Ramello said.

'Well, you've got tear emojis wherever his stupid name is,' RD scoffed.

'I ain't telling you shit, and I can do whatever I please,' Ramello snapped, wiping a trickle of blood from his lip with the back of his hand.

RD delved into the WhatsApp; each click of the screen was an annoyance. He flicked through every contact, and then a smirk tugged at his lips when he landed on Edmond's contact. Ramello, still wiping away tears, watched as RD suddenly erupted into unstoppable laughter.

'What are you laughing at?' Ramello asked when he realised RD was looking at one of the messages Edmond had sent to him a long time ago.

RD ignored him, thumb swiping across the screen, lost in a world of memories.

Ramello sighed, the weight of the day settling on his shoulders. He leaned his head against the back of the sofa, seeking solace in its fabric. The room was dimly lit, the evening sun casting long shadows through the half-closed curtains.

Without warning, RD reached over and gently guided Ramello's head to rest against his shoulder. The touch was unexpectedly tender, and Ramello found himself leaning into it, inhaling the strong scent of RD's rich cologne.

'What are you doing?' Ramello's voice was soft, curiosity lacing his words. He watched as RD's eyes remained fixed on his phone screen, thumbs dancing across the glass surface.

RD didn't answer, lost in a digital world that seemed to hold his attention.

'How come you seem to be interested in Edmond's messages?' Ramello's voice held a hint of suspicion.

'Quiet, boy,' RD finally replied, his fingers absently ruffling Ramello's hair. 'I'm just lookin.'

'Can you stop being nosey?' Ramello's annoyance bubbled to the surface. RD's behaviour started getting on his nerves. One moment, he was distant and aloof; the next, he was being friendly and comforting.

'Can I ask you why one second you act like a psychopath killer,' Ramello continued, 'And then the next second you're being all nice?' The words spilled out, fuelled by frustration.

RD's lips curved into a smirk, but he remained silent. Ramello's patience waned. He leaned closer, his breath hot against RD's ear. 'Can you hear me?' he practically shouted.

In an instant, RD's hand shot out, fingers gripping his ear because of the high-pitched shout. 'You stupid boy,' he hissed, his gaze bearing into Ramello's eyes, dark and unyielding, 'What the hell are you playin' at? Ain't got time for chit-chat, so shut your trap before I rip that tongue out.'

Ramello silently settled back against the sofa, defeated, as RD returned to his phone. There was more to this puzzle; he was sure of it. But for now, he'd keep his questions locked away, waiting for the right moment for RD's secrets to unravel.

After a long while, RD turned his phone off and stretched, 'You packin' a whole universe in that pocket gadget; it's like a flea tryna lift a mountain,' he said.

'I brought it with my hard-earned money, so stop going on and on about my phone,' Ramello replied.

RD's laugh filled the room, a rare sound that echoed off the freshly painted walls, 'OK, but can ya now tell me who this Jeffery bloke is?' he asked, leaning back and studying Ramello's face.

'Jeffery is...is I don't know,' Ramello stammered hesitantly.

'Don't play with me, young blood,' RD said, his smirk deepening, 'Shall I tell ya who he is?'

Ramello looked at him, tears filling his eyes, 'Who?'

'How come you're tellin' me to tell you who he is when ya know yourself?' RD asked with a grin.

Ramello didn't reply; he just wiped his tears away from his eyes.

'He's your...' RD put his face closer to Ramello's ear and whispered like a snake ready to sting, 'Dad.'

Ramello burst into tears, 'Don't say that,' he shouted, 'I don't want to know anything about him.'

RD started to laugh mockingly and slapped his hand on his leg, 'You don't wanna know about Jeffery,' he taunted, 'Well, lemme tell ya, I'm gonna keep singin' his name from now on, it's like hot sauce on your wounds, and I'll be sippin' on your salty tears while you wail like a big ol' baby in those saggy diapers.'

Ramello moved away from RD, hatred boiling within him, 'You're just a devil,' he spat out.

Dalayza gasped, but RD laughed, 'I already told ya I vibe with that word.'

Ramello leaned his head on the arm of the sofa and closed his eyes. He just wanted to leave the house and live the way he used to with his brothers.

He felt RD's hand rest on his shoulder, 'Listen, boy,' RD said, 'I'm gonna bring a VIP who will brighten your life.'

'And who's that?' Ramello asked, sobbing.

'Surprise,' RD said with a wicked grin, 'But I assure ya, your moods gonna change; I already told Ace to bring the person; he should be arriving soon.'

Ramello wondered curiously who on earth he was talking about, probably an expert in the art of beating people up, who would knock the living daylights out of him.

'You stay here, boy,' RD said, then looked at his two children, 'Ander and Dalayza, come with me.'

Ramello watched as they walked out of the room, then he stood up, walked over to the mirror, and gasped at his reflection; his face did not look good.

He grabbed a tissue from his pocket and tried to wipe the blood away, but that was useless, so he sat back down, frustration overwhelming him.

Chapter 12
The VIP's Arrival

Ramello sat on the sofa for a while, his body feeling weak and trembling with pain. Suddenly, RD came charging into the room. He grabbed his car keys off the fireplace, glanced at Ramello, and smiled but said nothing. He then left the room with a strenuous walk.

Ramello leaned his head against his palm, eyes half closed, when he heard someone in the hallway.

'Ya did an outstanding job, ma boys,' RD laughed, walking back into the room with five men behind him. They were all laughing like madmen.

'Listen, Red Devil,' one of the men laughed, making Ramello cringe; he hadn't heard those words for ages, 'Do you know Ace's face got smashed up?'

RD laughed, 'He's my ride-or-die, my day-one, the one that's got my back like no other person has,' he declared, 'Where is he anyway?'

One of the men looked out the door and then back at RD. 'He's fighting with the lad.'

'Yo, slide over there before Ace gets a good bashin'?' RD barked.

The man bolted out of the room; RD turned towards Ramello. 'Your sunshine VIP, who I was tellin' ya about, just stepped into the house,' he sneered.

'I guess you mean life dulling,' Ramello retorted, irritated.

RD rolled his eyes and remarked, 'We will soon be bringin' the man to you,' he announced, departing from the room.

After a while, RD walked back into the room with Ace and the other man who had been sent to help him. Between them, there was another man who looked very angry. He looked around the room, scanning everything until his eyes finally fell on Ramello. They both looked at each other, recognising each other simultaneously.

'Ramello!' the man exclaimed.

'Edmond!' Ramello shouted in delight. He felt happy to see his brother, but he remembered that Edmond had gone against him and had joined VD. After thinking for a while, Ramello concluded that he also liked VD.

'How did you get here?' Ramello screeched with excitement.

'How do ya think he got here?' RD asked, lighting up a cig. 'We caught the little nipper; lovely family reunion,' he smirked, 'Sit down, Edmond.'

'Sit down where?' Edmond snapped.

'Near your bro,' RD laughed, stealthily approaching Edmond, their heights almost matching. With a deliberate motion, he exhaled an acrid cloud directly at Edmond, who coughed and squinted, momentarily blinded by the haze, 'You two can enjoy each other's company before I decide to press the trigger, and it's going to be lights out for both of you.'

Edmond looked at Ramello and then sat near him. They looked at each other for a while. Ramello couldn't believe his eyes; after such a long time, he had one of his brothers sitting near him.

'Don't move the pair of ya; I'll be back,' RD said, walking out of the room; the other men followed behind.

'Edmond,' Ramello smiled, but Edmond didn't look too happy. He just tapped his head with his hand and looked ahead.

'Edmond,' Ramello said, his voice shaking, 'Don't ignore me.'

'I'm listening,' Edmond sighed, his weariness evident.

'How come they brought you here?' Ramello asked.

'I don't know,' Edmond replied, staring at Ramello in the eyes, 'I've had enough of this shit.'

'Me too,' Ramello admitted, his frustration mirroring Edmond's. 'But I can't do anything about it, which only fuels my annoyance.'

Edmond put his arm around Ramello's shoulders, 'Can I ask you what happened to your face?' he inquired, concern etching his features.

'RD busted it, that's what,' Ramello answered bitterly.

The living room door swung open, and RD entered. He sat on the sofa opposite them and assessed Ramello, 'Is your heart at peace?' he asked with a smirk.

Edmond stared at him, hatred glowing in his eyes, 'You're so evil,' he spat, his words carrying a threat.

'Me being evil does not harm me. Actually, it makes me stronger,' RD smoothly remarked, putting his arms behind his head.

Edmond glared at him, 'Your evilness might not harm you, but my fist will,' he shouted, standing up and flinging himself at RD. He grabbed RD's meticulously styled hair, making him scream like a girl. He then tried to punch RD's face, but RD kept his face down, shielding it with his arms.

Edmond punched RD's stomach, only to make him laugh. Suddenly, Edmond screamed and fell to the floor, clutching his arm. Then, as if awakening from a nap, RD sat up, stretching like a cat. Ramello looked at RD's hands and realised he had a gun with a silencer. Ramello yelled in panic and ran over to Edmond, who was on the floor, blood seeping from his wounded arm. He knelt near him, tears in his eyes, 'Why did you do that?' he sobbed, ruffling Edmond's hair and giving RD daggers. He looked at the wound and realised that the bullet hadn't directly hit Edmond's arm; it had slightly grazed it but was bad enough to make Edmond's arm bleed severely.

'Dude should have tried to act his cool; he would have been fine; now he's playin' with fire,' RD laughed, twisting his life-threatening gun in his fingers like a fidget spinner.

Ramello started to feel hot and annoyed; he looked at Edmond's arm, which was still bleeding from the shot. His gaze shifted between his wounded brother and the devilish figure of RD, who was sitting calmly with a twisted grin.

Suddenly, the front room door opened, and Ander walked in. His eyes instantly went towards Edmond, who had lost consciousness.

'What's going on, Dad?' he asked with a sigh, sitting near his devilish dad.

RD's smile widened. 'I popped the lad for actin' like a headless chicken,' he replied, 'Tryna be like a bull, charging at me and messed ma hair up as well,' he commented, brushing his hair back with his hand.

Ander looked at Ramello, who was sobbing near his brother, 'Why's that guy crying like a big baby?' he wondered aloud.

Ramello looked up at him, wiped his tears away, jumped straight onto Ander and started beating him.

'Dad!' Ander's cry echoed through the room as Ramello's blows rained down. 'Can you help me and stop looking? I'm going to die.'

RD stood up, grabbed Ramello's arm, and flung him off Ander, making him scream as his head banged into the table. Ramello stood up; his head spun, but he wasn't going to leave RD alone.

'Challengin' me, boy?' RD asked, walking up to him, and slapping him across the face, sending Ramello into a twist of anger and shock.

RD laughed and was going to give him another slap when Ramello's eyes caught sight of RD's gun, which RD had left on the sofa. Ramello ran towards it, grabbed it and pointed it towards RD; he had never wielded a gun before, so he didn't know how to use it; all he knew was to pull something and shoot a bullet in whichever direction you wanted.

RD laughed and walked straight towards Ramello, who was busy trying to find a way of cocking it. 'You thick boy,' he laughed, 'Thanks for remindin' me about ma gun; now I'm 'bout to close the last chapter of your life, been waitin' on this moment since way back,' he tried to snatch it from Ramello, who had a firm grip on it and was trying his best to hold onto the gun. RD twisted Ramello's wrist, who screamed with pain and had to let go of it, 'Boy,' RD continued, 'It doesn't even have any bullets left in it; you're one Charlie, ain't ya?'

Ramello felt ashamed. He had hoped RD had gotten scared, but RD never seemed frightened. He looked at RD, who was loading a mag into the gun and smiling to himself. RD looked up at Ramello and laughed in his face, 'You thought you'd pulled some crazy stunt, huh? But you ain't even crossed the starting line. Now, watch me paint this room red.'

Ramello slumped onto the sofa and started to cry, 'Just do what you want with me; I don't care,' he shouted.

RD started to walk up and down the room, flinging his gun into the air and catching it. He then looked at Ramello, who had his head slumped on the sofa's arm and was loudly sobbing. RD was just about to say something when his phone started to ring. He stared at it for a while and then answered it. 'Hi, Winton,' he said sternly, 'I haven't heard from you in a while, so I'm wondering what ya want from me.'

Ramello tried his best to listen to the conversation but couldn't make out anything because the volume was too low; he gave up and sat on the floor near Edmond.

'You watch!' RD screamed to the person who was on the phone, 'I'm going to come and gun you down; why did you let that guy slip through our fingers? You know there's no second chance man!'

The man on the other side started to scream back, but then RD cut him off, 'Shut your gob,' he yelled, 'Don't clown around with me and quit spittin' that weak sauce. Your daft excuses? Straight trash, man! That dude's got the whole block buzzin'. Some say he's cookin' up schemes in the shadows, movin' like a ghost. Others swear he's got connections all the way to the top; keep your eyes peeled 'cause he's playin' a different game, and we're all just pieces on his board.'

The person slammed the phone down. RD stared at it for a while, fuming with anger, and then slipped it into his pocket. He looked up at the clock; anger could be seen written all over his face.

Ramello stood up, walked up to him, and held his hand, 'Listen,' he said in a low voice, hoping he would listen to him.

RD turned his gaze to him, 'What is it, you wretched boy?' he snapped; his words were like a whip, lashing out venom.

Suddenly, Ramello didn't want to speak to him; he was already being awful, 'Nothing actually,' he mumbled, hoping RD would ignore him.

'You better tell me before I smash your face,' RD thundered, digging his fingers into Ramello's arm and dragging Ramello down to sit near him.

Ander stood up and looked at his dad, 'I'm going outside,' he said, walking out of the room and leaving RD and Ramello in their fractured world. RD looked into Ramello's eyes, 'Spill the beans or catch these hands, young blood,' he said, his hands close to Ramello's face, ready to hit him; he did not move his gaze away from Ramello.

Ramello started to feel worried. 'Nothing, I just wanted to...to...' he stammered. RD sighed and grabbed Ramello's face. 'Tell me before I remodel that grill of yours,' he demanded. The threat hung heavy, a promise of violence.

'Nothing,' Ramello managed to choke out, but his voice was muffled as RD's fingers continued to crush his face forcefully. His face felt like clay, being reshaped against his will.

'Listen, lad,' he said gruffly, 'I have information that's getting to my head, and it's bloody pressing my gas pedal. Do you understand? It's getting me furious as well.'

Ramello's mind raced; RD's mood swings were as unpredictable as lightning strikes. One moment, he was a tempest; the next, a calm sea. 'And what is it that's making you go mental?' Ramello ventured, not knowing what else to say.

'The thick-headed fool who called me claimed that he spotted your pops, the same knucklehead I've been chasin' for ages.' RD said with a loud sigh, 'My man said that your dad was driving a white SUV, and this is the point which makes me go bonkers; he didn't even bother jotting the damn number plate down, neither did he peep the make of the whip, Man, that's some next-level frustration right there!' RD's hand tightened on Ramello's arm, a silent plea for answers.

'How am I meant to help?' Ramello asked.

RD sighed and brushed his hair back, 'I don't need your kiddish help,' he replied, 'I'm just trying to cook up a plan, a way to finally corner that slippery idiot.'

Ramello nodded and was just about to say something when someone knocked on the door. RD stood up and walked up to the window. He looked out, then sighed, 'That spazza has come, probably to throw a tantrum about me shouting at him on the phone,' he said, walking out of the room. Ramello sat beside Edmond, who was waking up, 'Are you all right?' he asked.

'Does it look like it?' Edmond groaned loudly, 'My arm is killing me, and it might decide to part ways with the rest of me! I'm so lucky that it just skimmed me.'

'Don't talk too loudly, Ed. You're busting my ears,' Ramello murmured. 'Come, let's make you sit on the sofa.'

Ramello helped Edmond sit on the sofa and then sat near him, 'I hope your arm gets better,' he said, looking at Edmond's grumpy face.

After a bit, RD returned to the room with another man behind him who was already screaming his head off.

'Yo, Winton,' RD said, his voice a low growl as he sat near Ramello, 'I ain't got a clue which language you're spittin'; park your ass on the sofa and speak to me like a regular human.'

Winton eased himself onto the sofa, positioning himself directly opposite RD; he glanced at Ramello and Edmond but didn't say anything, 'As I was saying,' he began, 'How was I meant to take the bloody number plate down when the lunatic whizzed through the street like a bat on fire?'

'Use your blind eyes, that's what,' RD thundered and turned his gaze towards Ramello, 'Go fetch me a glass of water before I break this bloke's face.'

Ramello nodded; he found it weird that RD told him to do something. He stood up and limped out of the room, still wincing with pain from the beatings. He wandered down the hall until he reached the kitchen. He walked in and saw Dalayza sitting at the table, flicking through her phone, which seemed bigger than her face.

She looked up at him and started to give him dirty looks, 'Hi, what are you up to?' she asked rudely.

'Your dad requested a glass of water,' Ramello replied. 'Before he introduces his mate's face to chaos.'

Dalayza rolled her eyes, stood up and fetched a glass of water. 'Here you are,' she said, passing Ramello the glass. Ramello left the kitchen and returned to the living room, where he could hear RD and Winton screaming at each other. He opened the door and could feel the tension in the room.

'Slide that water over ASAP before I unleash chaos up here,' RD screamed.

Ramello handed him the water, and RD gulped it down like a drain. After he had finished, he locked eyes with Winton, 'You spit out one more thing I don't like,' he warned, brandishing the glass, 'This is coming straight for your face,' he said, turning towards Ramello, 'You gonna park it or not?'

Ramello sat down, slightly away from him, but RD grabbed his arm and pulled him closer. Then he looked at Winton, 'You say something daft, and I'm going to throw you out of the window,' he hissed through clenched teeth.

Winton smirked; it was a fatal mistake. RD threw the glass at him. It shattered on his face, making Winton scream with pain and agony, 'Why did you have to do that?' he screamed out.

'I already had warned you,' RD yelled.

Winton glared at him but knew it was best not to argue anymore, 'Fine, so what do you want me to do for you?' he asked, crossing his arms.

'Get out of my house; that's what you can do,' RD answered coldly. Winton stood up and bolted out of the room, 'Are you going to open the door for me, or shall I break it down?' he shouted from the hallway. RD stood up and walked out of the room.

Ramello breathed a sigh of relief; he was glad RD hadn't done anything worse. He sat there for a while till RD came back into the room; he looked unhappy and sat down near Ramello, shutting his eyes, lost in thought.

'Are you alright?' Ramello asked after a while, observing the stillness in RD.

'Yes, I am. I was born for chaos,' RD replied, opening his eyes, 'What makes you ask, boy?'

'You are so silent that I thought you might have passed away,' Ramello teased cheekily, 'Just a joke.'

'You're lucky you said 'joke,' otherwise I would have taken care of you,' RD said, shutting his eyes again.

'Can I ask you something?' Ramello asked, curiosity tugging at him, 'What's your real name? I'm sick of this Red Devil stuff.'

RD's eyes flickered open, a rare smile playing on his lips, 'I didn't expect you to ask that,' he said, 'But I ain't hiding my name from anyone, so I'll tell you, it's Vincent Caruso.'

The name sounded no better than his gangster name, making Ramello shiver. 'Nice name,' he managed with a shaky smile. 'I don't want to mess with you. All I want is a straightforward answer, and I don't care what it will be.'

RD stared at him, 'What is it?' he asked, 'I hope it won't want me to break your face.'

Ramello sighed, 'I don't care if you take my head off; I just want a simple answer,' he replied.

'OK, get along with it, boy, before I fall asleep,' RD said, yawning and reclining on the sofa.

Annoyance flickered across Ramello's face, but he decided not to address RD's bad manners, 'I've already asked so many times, and you always give me cryptic answers,' he said, glaring at RD, who appeared to be dozing off. 'What are you going to do with me and my brother?'

RD looked at him and then sat up straight, 'I knew you'd ask that,' he laughed, 'I'm going to keep you inside my house till I get my hands on your stuck-up dad.'

'And what are you going to do with Edmond?' Ramello asked. He didn't understand why Edmond was getting involved in all this rubbish.

RD laughed, 'You don't worry about him; focus on yourself,' he said, glancing at Edmond, who shot him a dirty look.

'So, what's your plan for me?' Edmond asked, 'I don't even know who you are and what you are.'

'I'm a human,' RD laughed.

'No, you're an animal,' Edmond scoffed, 'You don't even look like a human; you're a talking animal.'

RD looked at him with a smile, 'You lot really think calling me names is going to change your cursed lives or bother me?'

Edmond looked like he would have broken RD's face if his arm hadn't been shot. He was lucky it wasn't bleeding too much.

'Listen, lads,' RD said, looking at both of them, 'You might as well relax and just keep it in your minds that you're not going anywhere.'

Ramello and Edmond stared at him with annoyance, 'Fine,' Edmond grumbled, crossing his arms.

RD narrowed his eyes and started to think, 'You two stay here, I need to go,' he declared, striding out of the room.

Edmond and Ramello spoke for a while until Ander came into the room, 'What are you weirdo's doing?' he asked, walking towards one of the drawers.

Ramello glared at him, 'You shut your gob; you should be ashamed of even talking to people because you've got a horrible dad who shot you in the leg, and you're a lucky man that you are still walking; I guess the person who fixed your leg thought you were a robot, or some hard stone, we should call you 'Mountain Man', you rocky beast,' he laughed.

Ander eyes blazed with anger, 'Listen, you snobby boy,' he spat through clenched teeth, 'Shall I tell you about the secret behind why I got shot?'

Ramello stared at him, 'What?' he snapped.

'I got shot trying to save you,' Ander shouted, 'And you are so horrible as well.'

'Stop talking rubbish,' Ramello shouted, 'And why would you want to save me? You're as bad as your bloody dad!'

'Because I wanted to,' Ander shot back, 'You just don't appreciate anything.'

'How am I supposed to appreciate anything when I wasn't aware of your kindness?' Ramello said, 'If you cared so much for my lovely life, why did you beat the living daylights out of my face? I'm still in pain; I feel like I'm about to die.'

'Because if I didn't, I would have got shot again,' Ander replied.

Edmond watched them debate for a while and then said, 'Can you stop debating? You sound so stupid.'

Suddenly, the living room door opened, and RD stormed in, 'What the bloody hell's goin' on?' he roared, 'I could hear you lot hollerin' from my bleedin' bedroom.'

'Ander was being rude to us when he walked into the room,' Ramello explained.

'Ramello started to scream his face off for no reason,' Ander shouted back.

'You lot are so pathetic,' RD sighed, 'Ander, can you scoot out of the room and not talk to them?'

Ander rolled his eyes, grabbed whatever he wanted from the room and stomped out. RD sighed, turning towards Ramello and Edmond, 'Make sure you don't do anything daft,' he said, walking out of the room and banging the door behind him.

Chapter 13
The Unveiled Secret

RD gave Edmond and Ramello a spacious room with two neatly arranged beds for the night.

When Ramello woke up, it was midnight. He looked at Edmond, who was still fast asleep. He stood up and walked over to him; his pain from all the beatings he had felt like a hot, sharp knife that had sliced him throughout his body, and as if a bolt of lightning had struck his body from head to toe, sometimes he felt like he was having trouble breathing, and sometimes feeling a sharp, stabbing pain in the head where most of the punches had landed. He could see his face in a mirror nearby; it had started to turn bluish. 'Edmond,' he whispered, sitting near him, 'Wake up.'

Edmond's eyes shot open, 'What are you doing?' he asked, sounding very alert as if he wasn't even asleep, 'It's midnight, and you're walking around as if you're not even tired or injured. Get some sleep; you'll need it.'

'Edmond, we can't stay in this house; let's make a run for it,' Ramello replied, only to make Edmond laugh, dismissing his idea as folly.

'Don't be naïve, we'll get caught, and how would that be possible? The place is probably on lockdown,' Edmond asked.

'I'm going to get out of this house, that's what,' Ramello responded with determination.

Edmond sat up in his bed and put his arm around Ramello's shoulders, 'My dear younger brother,' he said, 'I don't think we should risk that.'

Ramello rested his head on Edmond's shoulder, 'I don't know what to do; my life is ruined,' he sobbed.

'Don't say that', Edmond said, 'We'll find a way out of this terrible ordeal.'

'I want my dad,' Ramello choked out, 'Why is he not here to solve my problems? Why is he not here to witness my tears? Why is he not here to comfort me?'

'Listen, Ramello, Dad knows everything about you, so don't worry,' Edmond said, trying to cheer him up.

'Can you repeat what you just said?' Ramello asked.

'What do you want me to repeat?' Edmond asked, puzzled.

'Why did you say 'dad'? You don't even know my dad,' Ramello asked, annoyed, 'He's my dad, not yours.'

Edmond's blue eyes glistened with tears, 'Of course, he's also my dad, and you're my younger brother,' he replied.

Ramello took his head off Edmond's shoulder and stared at him, gobsmacked, 'What does that mean? We've been living together for years, and nobody told me that you're my real brother. Are you lying?' he asked.

Edmond wiped his tears away and put his hands around Ramello's face, 'I was not allowed to tell you?' he confessed.

'Why, what was the problem?' Ramello asked, he couldn't believe Edmond was his blood brother.

'When our adoptive dad was going through the process of adopting us, it was a time filled with hope and uncertainty. He initially expressed a preference for adopting only me, and I remember feeling a mix of excitement and fear. But then, some other legal requirements had to be fulfilled, and he had to adopt both of us. However, behind closed doors, our adoptive dad revealed his true feelings. He made it clear that he favoured me over you. He warned me not to reveal our true relationship to you and told me to keep it hidden if I wanted him to continue treating me kindly,' Edmond explained, 'But these gangsters seem to believe that you are aware of our true relationship, that's why the peculiar RD asked if your heart was at peace.'

'I don't understand why our adoptive dad didn't like me,' Ramello said, tears filling his eyes.

'Don't worry about that,' Edmond responded. 'At least you know you've got me by your side,' he murmured, running his hand through Ramello's brown hair, and kissing him on the forehead.

Ramello suddenly looked up at him, 'So, are we going to try to get out of this house or not?' he asked hopefully.

Edmond looked at him nervously, 'If we get caught, then what?' he asked.

'Then we will get slaughtered; who says our lives are a bed of roses anyway,' Ramello replied with a grin.

'And after we leave the house, where will we go?' Edmond asked, tilting his head to one side, 'We don't even know where the keys are.'

'About the keys, I know where they are; RD always keeps them near the front door, and about where to go, don't worry, at least we'll be free,' Ramello smiled, his eyes gleaming with determination, 'So, are you coming or not? I'm going.'

Edmond smiled happily, suddenly stood up, grabbed Ramello's hand, and helped him stand up. 'Of course, I'm coming with you.'

They winked at each other and then crept out the door into the vast, dark hallway. 'I'm sure everyone is asleep, so it shouldn't be too bad,' Ramello whispered, his stomach twisting in fear. He didn't know if this was an act of bravery or stupidity.

They silently walked down the dark hallway towards the front door. They slipped on their trainers and then looked at each other. 'Do you think this is a good idea?' Edmond whispered to Ramello, who looked like he had seen a ghost.

'It should be fine,' Ramello whispered back, gulping nervously.

Ramello quietly took the key from the hook. Very slowly, he slid it into the lock and gently turned it. The door slowly clicked open. Ramello peered outside, his heart pounding with fear that he might see somebody. Fortunately, nobody was around; they walked into the garden, relief and joy flowing through their bodies.

'Edmond,' Ramello murmured, 'RD's car isn't in the driveway.'

'That means he must have gone somewhere,' Edmond whispered, his breath visible in the chilly air, 'We need to get out of here quick!'

They slipped out of the garden and hurriedly walked down the street, where they saw a black, polished car parked on the curb, its interior lights illuminating the darkness around it. They peered at the vehicle and saw RD occupying the driver's seat. He was looking down at his phone and smoking like usual with all the car windows down. His eyes, sharp as daggers, suddenly locked onto them, making them freeze in their place. He resembled a devil more at night with his contact lenses.

'Run!' Edmond screamed; they both turned around and started running.

RD flung his SUV's door open and started to chase them down the street, 'Get back here, you sly little nippy rascals! You're both just like your dad,' he bellowed, his voice echoing through the empty street.

After a lengthy chase, Edmond and Ramello started to tire; exhaustion and tiredness started slowing their pace while RD steadily got closer, his lanky legs giving him a significant advantage.

'Ramello, keep your pace up,' Edmond panted but was slacking himself.

Suddenly, Ramello ran into someone. Edmond heard a noise of someone falling; he quickly glanced back and saw Ramello sprawled on the ground. He stopped and looked at the man whom Ramello bumped into. The man was staring at them without moving his gaze. As this distraction continued to linger, RD caught up to them and seized the opportunity; he suddenly sprinted and flung himself into the air with his right leg outstretched, hitting the man viciously in the face and ending it with a well-practised tornado kick. The man fell onto the ground, with both hands clutching his face.

The man screamed with agony and stood up, looking at RD in the eyes.

'Oh! No, you don't,' RD smirked, 'I ain't interested in your baby rhymes; I ain't no ankle-biter you're tryna tuck into bed and lull to sleep, and anyway, what are you doing around here?'

'I was waiting for my friend to pick me up,' the man growled.

'Forget about your buddy's ride; I gotchu covered,' RD laughed.

'And how are you going to help me?' the man asked.

RD came closer, his eyes gleaming. 'Behold! The Tornado Kick Express!'

'What does that mean?' the man asked.

'It's simple,' RD declared, striking a pose. 'I'll unleash ma Tornado Kick, and you'll be whisked away to your destination. Hospital? Moon? Doesn't matter! All aboard the Tornado Kick Express!'

'And how does that work?' the man asked.

RD smiled, 'Step one: Spin. Step two: Kick. Step three: Skyrocket to the heavens.'

'You're totally loco,' the man said, rubbing his temple.

'I haven't exactly finished yet,' RD continued, 'It's eco-friendly as well, ma bro, zero carbon emissions.'

Ramello stood up, brushing dirt off his clothes, and looked at the two men who were going to fight, 'VD, what brings you here?' he asked, recognising the man RD was arguing with, 'How did you get out of the hospital?'

Edmond looked at them and gulped; VD was the one who had kidnapped him and his brothers a little while ago.

VD looked at Ramello and then back at RD. 'You took Edmond off me, so I'm going make sure you pay a price for it.'

RD laughed, pulling his wallet out, 'Here ya go, I'll pay for him,' he taunted, showing VD one cent.

VD glared at him, 'Don't try to take the rip out of me; you're going to pay a heavy price for everything you have done to me. Come on, fight me, you idiot, you will never win, I promise you,' he shouted, 'And I'm going to take both boys with me.'

RD smirked and put his wallet back into his pocket, 'Challenging me, are ya?' he mockingly laughed, walking closer to VD, 'Give it a shot, you grandpa.'

'Who says I'm a grandpa? I'm one year younger than you, and I don't even have any kids,' VD scoffed, 'You're bouncing about like you're in your youth.'

'I am still a spring chicken, ya know, rollin' smooth in ma youth; I'm only thirty-three,' RD smirked, 'But I doubt you even know how to count years. I'm sure ya skipped maths class,' he said with a fake laugh.

The situation started to get heated. RD kept making a complete mockery of VD and dancing around him like he was on a stage.

'Stop acting like a child,' VD yelled, 'Before I smash your ugly face up.'

'That's the whole point, mate,' RD laughed, 'I want ya to come at me, smash ma handsome face, then I'll give ya a school lesson on how it's properly done, ya wimp.'

'We've known each other since we were kids, and you've always been a filthy idiot,' VD shouted.

'Filthy idiot?' RD said, raising an eyebrow, 'Yeah, that's me, fam.'

'Yeah,' VD nodded, 'Also, you've just got a big gob, and definitely, you're no action; you're just good at bouncing around the streets trying to instil fear in people's hearts.'

'That's what I like doing, you stupid fish,' RD sneered, 'But let me tell ya something, I'm about to teach thoughtless morons like you a lesson. Mark my words: cross my path, and you'll be beggin' for mercy!'

'Come on then,' VD responded, walking towards RD and pushing him backwards.

RD stumbled a little and then cackled, making VD angry with his cool attitude, 'Come for me, and I'll knuckle your mug,' he spat.

Edmond looked at Ramello, who was still rubbing the injuries on his face, which he had received when he had gone head-on with VD. 'Do you know what?' Ramello said, 'That guy is made from steel. It feels like my nose has popped out of the back of my head.'

'Ramello,' Edmond whispered, 'Are we going to stay here and stare at their faces, or are we meant to do something? We're like extras in an action movie, no talking, no stunts, just awkwardly standing around.'

'I don't think I can run anymore; I'm so tired,' Ramello replied with a sigh, 'I might die if I try.'

'So, you're just going to watch these two fight?' Edmond asked. They both looked at each other till they heard VD scream. They turned their gazes and saw VD on the floor with RD standing on top of him, calmly staring down at him; VD continued to scream his head off with agony and distress.

'Bruv, quit barkin'!' RD growled, spitting on VD's face, 'You're yappin' like a bloody starvin' beast.'

'You're the one who's acting like a bloody hungry animal,' VD panted, wiping the spit away from his face and sitting up, 'You watch what I'm going to do with your face, you daft fool.'

'Aw! Your words have pierced my delicate soul,' RD said in his typical voice. He kicked VD in the face, who howled with pain, 'So, what's it gonna be? Shall I keep smashin' your mug, or are ya gonna man up and face me?'

VD glared at him and then stood up, 'I'm going to make a pulp out of you,' he said, grinding his teeth as if they were stubborn coffee beans.

RD rolled his eyes, 'I'm gonna kill ya and toss ya to the lions,' he said sarcastically, 'Listen, Lysander Vale, stop chattin' rubbish and let's get to the point.'

'Don't call me by my name,' VD snapped, 'I can't handle hearing it coming out of your dirty, filthy mouth, and anyway, what's your ridiculous so-called point?'

RD narrowed his eyes, tilting his head to one side. 'Can I toss a question your way? Why am I wasting my time fighting you, mate, when I've got bigger fish to fry?' he said, glancing at Edmond and Ramello.

'You're not leaving till you give the boy back to me,' VD said, 'You're just good at causing problems and, Vincent, gratitude is not in your vocabulary.'

'Gratitude?' RD smirked, 'What do I care? You're leaving without the lad.'

'No, I'm not,' VD answered, 'I'm going to do whatever it takes to get him back.'

RD, the master of exasperated sighs, leaned against the graffiti-covered wall. 'Listen, bruv,' he drawled, 'I'm not releasin' anyone until you scratch ma back.'

'And what's the job?' VD asked.

'Dead simple,' RD replied, his grin as sharp as a broken bottle. 'Bring me Salvatore. And guess what? I'm the one who's going to pull the trigger if he doesn't disclose info. Ta-da!'

'This is a difficult request,' VD responded, 'You're asking for the impossible. Why not send your lackeys? They're probably better than me in carrying out this mission.'

'If you fetch him for me, we won't need the boys, and we won't need to scrap over them. I'll get my answers out of Salvatore,' RD replied.

'Listen,' VD sighed. 'I'm telling you, this is a difficult task for me. I just told you I can't.'

'Little bro,' RD smiled. 'I don't even need him; I need his phone, and then I'll have all the info about Ramello's stupid dad on the table.'

VD's laughter erupted, 'Little bro?' he chuckled. 'You haven't called me that in years. But congrats, you've just made an impossible task even more impossible. How do I nab his phone? I'd rather drag Salvatore here himself.'

Ramello and Edmond, listening attentively to this unusual drama, were both left speechless and shocked to learn that RD and VD were actually brothers.

There was a loud laugh behind them, and someone said, 'Your wish is standing right behind you.'

RD and VD spun around, and then RD spoke loudly in a horrible tone, 'Salvatore, you maniac.'

Chapter 14
Secrets Of The Undercover Mansion

RD's eyes widened with hatred, his lips narrowing, and his right hand moved swiftly, brandishing a gleaming pistol.

Salvatore laughed, drawing his pistol from his cross-draw holster. 'Do you really think you'll extract the info from me? I'll die, but I'm never giving you the answer,' he said.

'Then I'll ensure your demise,' RD shouted.

'Listen, you guys,' VD said, breathing irregularly, his limbs trembling and slowly backing away, 'I'm not part of this; you hear me all.'

'You're nuffin' but a shaky lil' rodent,' RD bellowed at VD. 'Shoulda picked up a mic, mate. Singin' tunes would've lined your pockets better.'

'Bye guys, I'm not getting involved,' VD managed a smile, then ran off.

RD rolled his eyes and looked at Salvatore, 'Back off before I put a bullet through you.'

'Actually, you better back off before I make you into mincemeat,' Salvatore replied, 'Do you think I'm scared of you? I'm not going to hide in corners like your brother; I'm standing right before you, so if you want me, come for me.'

RD glared at him, 'Listen up, ain't nothin' gonna happen to ya if you spill the beans on where that scum of earth's hidin',' he said, grinding his teeth together.

'I don't understand why you want him so much; what's the problem?' Salvatore asked.

'Look, ya ain't blind to this issue,' RD said, his voice getting louder, 'So, quit spoutin' nonsense.'

Salvatore threw his gun into the air, catching it effortlessly, 'Let the two kids go, then I'll tell you what you want to know,' he proposed, a sly smile playing on his lips.

RD thought for a moment, then replied, 'Don't try to fool me, I remember when ya played me back in the days, and I ain't forgettin' ya promised that you were gonna give me an answer to somethin', but ya left me hangin' high and dry.'

Salvatore let out a guilty laugh, 'You've got me pegged, don't you?' he admitted, 'And that means we're due for a showdown.'

RD walked over to him with his hand on the gun's trigger, 'Look, you better bounce before I shoot ya,' he said through clenched teeth.

Salvatore smirked as a car sped into the road, nearly colliding with a nearby lamppost. As it screeched to a halt, Officer Jacob jumped out, 'Put down your weapons,' he demanded.

'Take the kids and get out of here, RIGHT NOW!' Salvatore shouted. But just then, RD shot a bullet at him, but luckily, it missed by millimetres.

Taking advantage of the commotion unfolding in front of them, Ramello and Edmond sprinted towards the car, but RD's sharp eyes noticed everything; he swiftly ran towards Ramello and roughly grabbed him by the arm. 'You're not goin' anywhere,' he hissed, looking at him with wicked eyes.

'You better let the boy go,' Salvatore yelled. He fired a bullet at RD, which hit him directly in the leg. The noise of the gunshot echoed through the street, and the scent of gunpowder hung heavy. As RD fell, he dragged Ramello down with him, his arm tightly around Ramello's neck, making it difficult for him to breathe.

Salvatore rushed towards them and tried to pull Ramello free, but he was trapped in a tight headlock and was gasping for air. 'Take the other boy; this one stays with me,' RD hissed.

'Let him go, NOW!' Salvatore warned, but RD didn't want to listen and pulled a knife from his jeans pocket. The knife gleamed in the dim light, its sharp blade pressing against Ramello's throat, 'Ya come any closer, and I'm gonna kill him.'

Tears welled inside Ramello's hazel eyes, 'Just leave me with him; it doesn't matter,' he sobbed, desperation clear on his face.

Officer Jacob stepped forward, 'We're not leaving you with this horrible beast,' he declared, his sharp, light-brown eyes angrily locked on RD.

Ramello's gasps grew desperate as RD's grip tightened around his neck, his every heartbeat a plea for freedom.

Torn between duty and compassion, Salvatore felt the weight of this never-ending nightmare. Rescue or risk? The choice hung like a blade over their heads.

'Just leave me with him; I don't want any more blood or destruction,' Ramello pleaded.

Salvatore's heart started pounding heavily in his chest; the weight of this horrible situation continued to pressurise him. He looked at Officer Jacob; it was the first time in his life he felt helpless. Attempting any rescue mission would get Ramello killed, and leaving Ramello with RD was not safe either; the most appropriate thing to do in these tense moments was to shoot RD, but there would also be a risk that if the bullet missed, RD would still attempt to stab Ramello.

RD's eyes bore into him, a menacing glare, 'If you come any closer, then I'm gonna kill the boy,' RD warned as if he had read Salvatore's mind. Salvatore suddenly realised that RD was holding Ramello so tightly that he was very close to choking him to death.

'I'll give you the guy's number, and then you can talk to him,' Salvatore said, a sense of fear and panic in his voice.

RD started applying more pressure to Ramello's neck, 'Just look at the boy and tell yourself that if you try takin' him, then I'm gonna kill him, and it's gonna be the last time ya will see him.'

Ramello looked at Salvatore, tears flowing down his cheeks, 'Quit playin' cry-baby, kid,' RD said, 'Ain't the moment for waterworks.'

RD slowly sat up, wincing with pain from the gunshot wound in his leg; Ramello still in his grasp, he locked eyes with Salvatore and then said with a weary sigh, 'Inform Under G that I'm gonna back off from the homie, but there's one catch: Under G gotta throw some cash ma way for takin' out ma lil' bro back in the day, ya dig?' He declared.

Salvatore glared at him. 'You must stop bringing that subject up because it was your fault for clashing with Under G, and then your little brother walked in the middle of it and got shot by mistake,' he replied.

'Phone him and lemme speak to him,' RD demanded, his face showing anger.

Salvatore pulled his phone out of his pocket and dialled a number. Under G answered. Salvatore started to talk to him, and after a lengthy conversation, he put the phone on speaker mode so RD could speak to Under G.

'Hi,' RD barked, every syllable dripping with menace.

'Hello, Vincent. What's the reason for this call?' Under G inquired, his voice calm as if he were discussing the weather.

Ramello was also listening to the conversation; it sounded like someone he had heard before.

'I phoned ya to tell ya I've got Ramello in lockdown. This is ma last warning. If ya slide me some good dosh for ma lil' bro ya took out back in the days, Ramello walks free. But if ya say 'no,' I'm gonna ice him right here and now,' RD said. It seemed like he was going to punch the phone, wishing the man on the other side would feel it.

Under G hesitated, then laughed, a mocking sound which grated on RD's nerves, 'I'll give you half a cent, you loser.'

'I'm serious,' RD bellowed, 'Cut the nonsense and tell me what your decision is.'

'If I compensate you for the death of your brother, I know you will still be after me; our history of conflict goes beyond this particular incident,' Under G replied.

Suddenly, RD screamed with pain as someone sneakily kicked him in the head, making him lose grip of Ramello. Ramello hastily stood up, gasping for air like a fish that the ocean's waves had tossed onto a beach. He quickly looked around his surroundings to see who had kicked RD and noticed with relief that it was Edmond.

'Good job, boy,' Salvatore laughed and looked at RD, who was holding his head with pain that was caused by the vicious kick he had received, 'You two get into Officer Jacob's car,' Salvatore ordered.

'What's going on?' Under G asked.

'Nothing; we're on our way,' Salvatore said, disconnecting the call. He looked towards Ramello and Edmond, nervously sitting in the car.

'How come they're sitting in my car?' Officer Jacob asked, 'I don't even know where you want me to take them.'

Salvatore sighed, 'I'll take them in my car if you're not feeling comfortable,' he said, looking at RD, whose battered body lay sprawled on the ground, groaning like a deflating balloon, 'I'll be a bit nice to you and put you on the sidewalk,' he said dragging RD onto the sidewalk.

He walked over to Officer Jacob's car, opening the back door where Edmond and Ramello were sitting, 'You two come with me; I'm taking you to my car; it's in the next street,' he said.

Ramello and Edmond jumped out of the car and started walking with Salvatore towards the next street, where Salvatore's black SUV was parked. They jumped into the car. Salvatore started the car and steered onto the main road. 'You're a lucky lad,' he said, looking at Ramello through the main mirror. I told you I would not save you again if you did something daft. Be grateful that I was driving by and saw you.'

Ramello nodded, then smiled, 'You're a gangster and a half.'

Salvatore grinned, 'I'm not the main gangster; I've got someone on top of me; everyone calls him Undercover Gangster; I work underneath him,' he said.

'Really, I didn't know that,' Ramello said.

'Well, now you know,' Salvatore replied, 'And I'm taking you to his house.'

Ramello's stomach churned; he was fed up with all these so-called gangsters. The only one he liked now was Salvatore. He looked at Edmond, who was dozing off in the seat next to him.

They were driving for an extended period when Ramello realised that Salvatore was taking them into the countryside, 'Where are you taking us?' he asked.

'Taking you to UG's house,' Salvatore replied, 'Nobody knows where he is because his house is hidden in the countryside.'

Ramello nodded; he understood what he was saying but started wondering who the gangster was.

After a long drive, Salvatore said, 'We've arrived.' Ramello gasped as he took in the sight before him; looming before him was a massive mansion, which some people would describe as 'You're in paradise.' Beautiful carvings adorned its façade, meticulously crafted with a delightful blend of lilac, red, and pristine white paint. It was like watching a fairy tale movie. It had beautiful, gorgeous greeneries and on the right side of its garden, an artificial waterfall cascaded, its glassy surface mirroring the moon. In the air, he could feel the freshness, openness and a slow breeze brushing against his face, combined with the night's warmth, which seemed to relax his mind. As his gaze continued to scan the lovely garden, flowers were everywhere, white and yellow, blossoming in the humid night; the petals of the roses were spread widely over the garden surface, giving out a sweet fragrance that lingered in the night breeze, spread far and wide. What a scenery it was!

Ramello turned towards Edmond and gently shook him awake, 'Come on, Ed, we're here,' he said, his voice filled with a mix of excitement and exhaustion.

Edmond groaned, his tired eyes fluttering open. 'I can't be bothered moving,' he mumbled, his voice heavy with sleep. He unbuckled his seatbelt and slowly stepped out of the vehicle, Ramello following suit.

Ramello was glad he was not in the car as he breathed in the warm air. They walked into the garden, and right in front of them was parked a gleaming white SUV in the corner of the garden. The number plate was proudly adorned with the letters 'UG LNY.'

As they approached the front door, Ramello noticed a network of strategically positioned IP security cameras encircling the house.

Salvatore's knuckles rapped gently against the front door, the sound echoing through the quiet night; Ramello and Edmond shifted nervously by Salvatore's side.

The front door swung open, revealing a young boy with a shock of raven-black hair and eyes that shone like sapphires. 'Hi, Kaily,' Salvatore greeted, his voice warm and familiar. 'Where's your dad?'

'He's in the living room,' Kaily replied, a shy smile forming on his face as his gaze shifted to Ramello and Edmond.

They stepped into the opulent mansion, a grandeur that could rival a regal palace. The air was heavy with the scent of wealth and privilege. Kaily led them through the living room, a space that could have been mistaken for a king's throne room. The ceiling soared to impressive heights, adorned with glittering crystal chandeliers. Yet, the room was bathed in a soft, muted glow from a solitary lamp tucked away in the corner. Velvet drapes framed tall windows, their folds cascading in graceful waves, their touch whispering against the polished floor. Ramello, drawn by curiosity, moved one of the velvet drapes and peered outside; the lush gardens beckoned, a symphony of emerald leaves, vibrant blooms, and moonlit pathways.

Ramello's eyes swept across the room, taking in every detail. They settled on a figure clad entirely in black, sitting on an armchair with a high backrest featuring beautiful decorations of flowers and leaves. He was wearing bright white trainers that rested on top of an elegant table; he seemed to be fiddling around with his phone. There was silence amid the lamp's soft glow; Ramello couldn't take his eyes away from the figure.

'I don't see any gangster,' Ramello finally voiced his frustration, 'All I see is Lenny.'

With a soft chuckle, Lenny pocketed his smartphone and straightened up, revealing his full self. 'Yes, I am Lenny, the one who was tasked with your safety, if you recall,' he said, a glimmer in his eyes that hinted at a deeper, more mysterious secret.

'You're the gangster, then?' Ramello asked.

'Yeah, I'm the undercover gangster,' Lenny sneered, his sharp words hanging in the air. He slightly shifted, removing his feet from the table, which was a small act of respect or perhaps a calculated move.

Lenny crossed the room towards them, his sky-blue eyes twinkling like distant stars and his straight brown hair falling elegantly over his forehead. He wore a silver ring on his left hand, and an expensive watch adorned his right wrist. He extended his hands towards Salvatore; their handshake was firm.

'You did a good job,' Lenny said, a rare smile spreading across his face.

But Lenny wasn't done; his gaze shifted to Ramello and Edmond, his smile warm and comforting, 'Hi, my lovely sons,' he murmured, his words a whisper meant only for them, a whisper that carried a promise of love and protection.

Caught off guard, Lenny staggered slightly as Edmond and Ramello enveloped him in a dual embrace.

Ramello's tears flowed freely as he asked, 'Are you actually our dad?'

'I am, my dear Ramello,' Lenny confirmed, his eyes locking into Ramello's, 'But make sure you don't call me 'Lenny' you have to call me 'Dad'.'

'But why did you abandon me?' Ramello uttered the question that had haunted him for years.

Lenny looked at him with sad eyes, 'I had never abandoned you,' he began, his voice like a fragile thread, 'I put you and your brother in the adoption centre because I believed it was the safest choice; too many people were after me and were threatening to hurt my family.' His confession was a plea for understanding.

Ramello's tears blurred the room, 'Safest?' he questioned, the words tasting bitter, 'But we still suffered; we still faced danger, did you not care?'

Lenny's touch was gentle as he wiped away Ramello's tears, 'I thought the adoption centre would shield you,' he confessed, 'I thought it could be a place where both of you could grow up without the weight of my sins.'

'But,' Ramello choked out, 'We were alone, lost and forgotten.'

Lenny's eyes held a lifetime of pain, 'I miscalculated everything,' he admitted, 'On many occasions, you both nearly died and have gone through a lot of mistreatment and pain, and for that, I will carry the burden of guilt and mistakes all my life.'

Ramello nodded with acknowledgement.

The room seemed to hold its breath, but then Lenny's resolve hardened. 'Now,' he said determinedly, 'From now on, both of you are going to stay in my house, and you will remain safe here.' He turned his gaze to Salvatore and continued, 'Salvatore is my cousin; call him 'Uncle', and Kaily is your stepbrother.'

'Let me tell you something else,' Salvatore said, eyeing Ramello, 'Do you know who RD and VD are?'

Ramello shook his head, 'No, all I know is that they're really evil and violent,' he responded.

'Why don't you tell them the real truth?' Salvatore suggested, glancing at Lenny, who met his gaze with a mix of understanding and concern.

As Lenny started to give an explanation to Edmond and Ramello, his expression softened. 'They're mine and Salvatore's distant cousins,' he said.

Ramello swallowed; now he understood why RD had weird mood swings and was so hesitant to kill him, and also VD had a similar personality.

'But how come they're so...' Edmond hesitated, searching for the right word.

'Horrible,' Lenny finished the sentence. His smile was grim, eyes reflecting memories, 'RD is worse than VD in everything.'

Ramello's mind raced, a whirlwind of emotions and questions. Suddenly, something hit his mind. Where was his mother in all of this? The urgency of the question pressed against his thoughts, threatening to consume him. He imagined her face, the warmth of her smile, the softness of her touch.

But before he could ask, Lenny sang to both of them, leaving his question unanswered:

'My dear sons, my pride, my heirs,
In this life of shadows, I swear,
You're the light, the hope, the dreams,
In the darkest night, the brightest beams.
I've walked through fire, through rain, through sin,
But for both of you, I'd do it all again.
You're the reasons I strive, I fight, I stand,
In this ruthless world, hand in hand.

I may be tough, maybe cold, maybe grim,
But for both of you, my heart sings a hopeful hymn.
Don't leave me, sons, stay by my side,
Together, we'll ride the tide with stride.
In my arms, you're both safe, you're both sound,

With my love, you're forever bound.
So, listen to my song, my solemn vow,
I'll protect you, sons! That's my avow!'

The moral of this story:

Amidst the tempests of life, when violence rages and storms threaten to engulf you, there remains an unwavering figure - the one man you can always look up to - your dad. For years, the protagonist believed his father had abandoned him, leaving him to navigate the chaos alone. Little did he know that his father, a hidden guardian, had put him in an adoption centre to shield him from danger. Beneath the veneer of abandonment lay a fierce protector, a gangster with a heart of gold. And so, through trials and problems, the protagonist discovers that the most unlikely protectors sometimes wear the darkest masks.

The protagonist finds out about his father's hidden life. He uncovers a secret underworld where violence is everywhere and danger lurks in every shadow. Yet, unexpectedly, his father's unwavering love and protection shine brightest in this darkness. The same hands that once clenched weapons now cradle the protagonist's dreams, shielding him from the storms that threaten to consume them both.

Remember, even in the midst of violence, love and sacrifice can emerge as unexpected guardians.

Always bear in mind that violence is never the solution. Its impact lingers long after the storms have passed, leaving scars that may never fully heal. True strength lies in safeguarding others without resorting to harm. When faced with difficulty, consider alternative paths that promote empathy, understanding, and compassion. By doing so, you not only protect others but also nurture a sturdier and more harmonious world.

Acknowledgement

I am profoundly grateful to my wife, whose steadfast courage and unwavering guidance have honed my writing skills. Her tireless support and unshakeable belief in my abilities have been indispensable on this journey.

Additionally, I am deeply grateful to my daughters, whose exceptional ideas have consistently inspired and enhanced my work. Their creative insights and encouragement have led to numerous breakthroughs and accomplishments.

Finally, I want to express my heartfelt appreciation to the rest of my family. Their unwavering support and belief in my potential have given me the strength and determination to pursue my dreams tirelessly. Their enduring encouragement and genuine desire for my success have motivated me constantly.

I am truly humbled and blessed to have such remarkable individuals in my life. Without their unwavering support, my achievements would not have been possible. Thank you all from the bottom of my heart.

Look out for book two from the Undercover Gangster Series!

Undercover Gangster Part Two

Ramello's life has settled into a comfortable rhythm. Years have passed since he has moved in with his estranged, long-lost father, and he rejoices in the warmth of their shared moments. Yet, beneath the surface, a persistent question gnaws at him: Where is my biological mother? He has no interest in his stepmum, although she is like a mum to him; she cares for him, and he greatly appreciates it, but his heart yearns for his actual biological mother.

One fateful day, his father approaches him with an unexpected proposition: to join the Secret Service. Ramello hesitates. It isn't the path he envisions, nor does he understand why his father doesn't suggest the idea to his elder brother, Edmond, who would have embraced the opportunity with open arms. Still, in a bid to please his father, Ramello agrees, following in the footsteps of his dad and his uncle, Salvatore.

As days pass, the weight of his unanswered question grows unbearable. Finally, he confronts his father, seeking clarity. Instead of explaining, his dad avoids it completely and gets angry every time he mentions or asks questions about his birth mother. Ramello's journey is about to take another sharp turn that will test his loyalty, unravel family secrets, and plunge him into a world of intrigue and danger. He realises that the Secret Service is more than a career choice; it is a gateway to revelations he never anticipated.

Ramello's curiosity grows more and more. He then notices a strange figure who seems to be lurking in the shadows, who wears a hoodie that perpetually conceals their face. He continues to see this person suspiciously walking around wherever he is. Their presence is dominant. Is it a mere coincidence, or is there a deeper connection to something hidden? Ramello can't shake off the feeling that this mysterious stranger might be the key to unlocking his answers. But who is it? Why are they following him? Will they know more about Ramello's past than he does himself? The truth is about to unravel, and his life is about to change.

Ramello's days at the Secret Service are intense. He trains rigorously, honing his surveillance, decryption, and covert operation skills. But amidst the adrenaline-fueled drills, there is a constant distraction: the hooded figure.

Every time Ramello steppes out onto the bustling streets of Washington D.C., the mysterious figure is always a few steps ahead of him, his face always obscured by the strange hoodie. Who is it? Why is Ramello being followed?

Ramello decides to investigate. One day, he deceives the figure and tails it through a crowded subway station, across dimly lit alleys and even into the heart of Meridian Hill Park. But each time he gets close, they disperse into thin air and are nowhere to be found. Their movements are fluid, almost supernatural. It is as if they anticipate his every move. Who is this person, and what other twists lurk in Ramello's path?

Stay Tuned for More Exciting Adventures!

Thank you for joining me on this thrilling journey. If you enjoyed this story, there's so much more waiting for you! Dive into a world of mystery, intrigue, and unforgettable characters with these upcoming titles:

- **Secret Gangster:** Unveil the hidden life of a man who walks the fine line between law and chaos, haunted by the loss of those he held dear.
- **Never Underestimate Girls!:** Discover the power, resilience, and grace of girls who refuse to be underestimated.
- **Triple Caste Gangster:** Follow the enigmatic smile that holds secrets capable of changing everything.
- **A Secret Hidden Behind Truth:** Unravel the layers of illusion to find the truth that lies beneath.

And that's just the beginning! Keep an eye out for even more captivating stories that will keep you on the edge of your seat!

Don't miss out!

Visit the website below and you can sign up to receive emails whenever Joseph Jethro publishes a new book. There's no charge and no obligation.

https://books2read.com/r/B-A-TDFLC-MXFBF

BOOKS 2 READ

Connecting independent readers to independent writers.